OLD TRANSVA

THE ANNIVERSARY EDITION OF HERMAN CHARLES BOSMAN

Planning began in late 1997 – the fiftieth anniversary of Bosman's first collection in book form, Mafeking Road *– to re-edit his works in their original, unabridged and uncensored texts. The project should be completed by 2005 – the centenary of his birth.*

GENERAL EDITORS:
STEPHEN GRAY AND CRAIG MACKENZIE

Already published in this edition:
MAFEKING ROAD AND OTHER STORIES
WILLEMSDORP
COLD STONE JUG
IDLE TALK: VOORKAMER STORIES (I)
JACARANDA IN THE NIGHT

Herman Charles Bosman

OLD TRANSVAAL STORIES

The Anniversary Edition

Edited by Craig MacKenzie

HUMAN & ROUSSEAU
Cape Town Pretoria Johannesburg

Back cover photograph of Herman Charles Bosman in Johannesburg,
by an unknown street photographer, courtesy of the Harry Ransom Humanities Research Center.
Two photographs of the Marico Hotel, before and after the Second Anglo-Boer War,
courtesy of the National Archives, Pretoria.

Design and typeset in 11 on 13 pt Times by ALINEA STUDIO, Cape Town
Printed and bound by NBD
Drukkery Street, Goodwood, Western Cape

ISBN 0 7981 4085 2

HERMAN Charles Bosman (1905–1951) was born near Cape Town but spent most of his life in the Transvaal, the region which provides the setting for almost all of his work. After a short stint as a teacher in the Marico Bushveld, a spell in prison for murder and a six-year sojourn in London and Europe, Bosman worked as a writer and editor on various newspapers and periodicals in the Transvaal.

Old Transvaal Stories is the most comprehensive gathering to date of Bosman stories that were not written in series – that is, 'non-Oom Schalk', 'non-Voorkamer' stories. These pieces were written intermittently between 1931, soon after Bosman was released from prison on parole, and the early 1950s, shortly before his death. They therefore represent twenty years of experimentation by Bosman with short fictional forms. Many of the stories are already well-known. Four of them, however, appear here for the first time and two others have never before been collected into book form.

Contents

Introduction

From the early 1920s, while still a schoolboy, up until the end of his life, Bosman experimented with various story forms. He achieved greatest success with his 'Oom Schalk Lourens' tales, memorable for their masterful use of a narrator figure, and his later 'Voorkamer' sequence, which uses multiple narrators in a 'conversation forum' format. *Old Transvaal Stories* gathers together the less well-known, but equally engaging, stories that make up a third category in his story-writing – stories in which Bosman becomes more personally involved as a narrator.

Productive and challenging as the Oom Schalk and Voorkamer sequences were for Bosman, they confined the author to a certain formula: a stable narrator (or set of narrators), a fixed setting and the kind of story one expects to hear in an oral, storytelling milieu. In *Old Transvaal Stories* we see Bosman revelling in the freedom of being able to experiment with stories of various kinds: very short narratives and sketches that nowadays would be called 'short shorts', longer pieces in which the narrator intrudes quite conspicuously and some in which an invisible narrator is used.

I have arranged these stories in a way that gives them a historical trajectory. The reader is taken from the uncharted Transvaal of the pioneering voortrekkers ("Jakob's Trek") to the hard, concrete environment of post-war Johannesburg ("'Onsterflike Liefde'", "Underworld") – a passage of over a hundred years. In between, we have a Boer folk-tale ("A Tale Writ in Water"), Boer War stories ("The Affair at Ysterspruit", "A Boer Rip van Winkel"), Bushveld local colour and 'skinderstories' ("The Heart of a Woman", "The Night-dress", "In Church", "Politics and Love", "New Elder", "Shy Young Man", "Night on the Veld"), and modernist retellings of hoary old tales ("Old Transvaal Story", "The Murderess", "Veld Story"). The short sketch "The Old Muzzle-loader" is a wistful, slightly wry look back at the trekker era before we are irrevocably in the urban, more sophisticated milieu of the long, metafictional "Louis Wassenaar." "The Clay-pit" is a final reworking of the embedded story in "Louis Wassenaar" about the orphan girl, and it brings the country into the city in a way that is full of forlorn pathos. The promise held out by the abundant open veld in

Zeerust before the turn of the century, in the days of the independent South African Republic. A scene that might have greeted the orphan girl in "The Clay-pit" when she returned to the Marico to testify at the trial of her former lover: "when the coach that brought her back from Kimberley stopped in front of the Transvaal Hotel, half the population of Zeerust saw her alight on to the pavement."

"Jakob's Trek" has been traded for a tawdry living on the night-streets of the city.

The element that binds all of these stories together is the ongoing, self-ironic commentary that Bosman conducts on the art of story-telling. Indeed, many of the stories are 'retellings' of tales heard so often that they have entered the store of oral folklore and as such are ripe for playful, humorous subversion. This aspect can be traced in each of the stories gathered here, but is most conspicuous in the one that gives this volume its name.

As its title indicates, "Old Transvaal Story" does not purport to be new. Indeed, the elderly raconteur who contributed to the same journals as Bosman, W. C. Scully, and his "Ukushwama" (1895), are acknowledged in the story's opening line, with a little transfer from the Transkei to the Transvaal; and there are other sources. "Old Transvaal Story" is also actually a rewriting of Bosman's earlier Oom Schalk story, "The Gramophone" (which first appeared in May, 1931), as he suggests. This story in turn apparently had its origins in Bosman's experiences in prison, where he encountered a fellow prisoner who had killed his wife

Another view of the Marico Hotel, Zeerust, this time in the early twentieth century, soon after the British occupation. (Photographer(s) unknown.)

and buried her under the dung floor of his dining room. The man was then beset by a group of his friends who sprang a surprise party and he was forced to go through with his bizarre pretence that his wife had gone away. This tale is recounted in "Rosser", a Bosman story first published posthumously in 1958 in *The Purple Renoster*, the literary magazine edited by Lionel Abrahams.

A still earlier potential source is Edgar Allan Poe's "The Tell-tale Heart" (first published in 1845), in which a clearly deranged first-person narrator recounts his minutely planned and executed murder of an old man who lives with him. It is very likely that Bosman had read Poe's story, given his enthusiasm for the author, and this influence may partly account for Bosman using a variation of the tale. However, as Bosman's own references to Scully's "Ukushwama" and the Transvaal's "only ghost story" suggest, the tale probably has variations in numerous folk traditions in various parts of the world, and is therefore not 'original' to any one writer.

What Bosman does in this story is artfully merge a discussion of the Transvaal's "only ghost story" and its "only murder story" with a variation of his own on these 'many-told' tales. The passage of the fifty-odd years between Scully's story and Bosman's retelling has some in-

The Abe Berry illustration that accompanied the first publication of "Old Transvaal Story" (On Parade, *3 Sept., 1948*)

teresting effects on the narrative texture of the tale. Where Scully's story is told as a fairly ingenuous piece of local colour, in Bosman's rendering the artifice of the tale is foregrounded. Bosman sends up the genre of the 'ghost story': his conversational, light-hearted tone runs directly counter to the atmosphere that traditionally envelops a rendering of the tale, and where the storyteller would normally attempt to conjure up suspense in the opening part of his tale, Bosman addresses the reader directly. He eschews the customary device of his raconteur Oom Schalk, and so lures the reader into believing that a discursive rather than narrative piece will unfold. Of course, towards the end of the piece Bosman changes gears and the story ends climactically.

Of interest, then, are the overtly metafictional aspects in Bosman's rendering of the tale. The merging of genres (discursive, fictional) is only one example of this. Bosman is also supremely conscious of the impossibility of being entirely original in the telling of a story: a story one tells is inevitably a reconstitution of stories that go before it, as Bosman implicitly acknowledges here. What remains to the writer, therefore, is the self-conscious redeployment of pre-existing materials, a process Bosman puts into practice with consummate mastery in this story.

The process of 'retelling' can be traced in virtually all of the pieces in this volume. The tale of the orphan girl who is abused by her step-father is told twice here (in an embedded, reflexive form in "Louis Wassenaar" and in a more final, achieved form in "The Clay-pit"); indeed, it is introduced by the narrator of "The Clay-pit" as an old story that has done the rounds for years. Similarly, "A Tale Writ in Water" is prefaced by the remark that it has been told to the narrator "a number of times, it being of a legendary nature." At the start of "A Boer Rip van Winkel" the narrator comments that he is often "surprised to find what a very old tale it was that has kept me from the chimney corner." This comes as an agreeable surprise, he adds, for he has "a preference for old tales." The tale itself is of course a local variation of Washington Irving's famous "Rip van Winkle" (1845).

A portrait of Scully by D. C. Boonzaier ('Nemo') (The Sjambok, *10 Jan., 1930*)

*Two views of a still-functioning clay-pit in the Marico District, 1998
(photos: Craig MacKenzie)*

There are other areas of interest that Bosman found when he was devising short stories more loosely. In "New Elder", "Shy Young Man" and "Night on the Veld", for instance, we can see Bosman working on what would become his 'Voorkamer' formula: a set of narrators who frequently find themselves in each other's company and while away the time telling tall tales. This became such a successful recipe that Bosman would end up writing eighty such pieces.

Something else of interest is Bosman's sustained exploration of the morbid, rather Gothic currents that run beneath the tranquil somnolence of rural life ("The Heart of a Woman", "The Night-dress", "In Church" and "The Murderess"). He might have made his name by writing redolently and sometimes lyrically about matters bucolic, but he was not blind to the dark underside of life on the platteland. "The Affair at Ysterspruit" contains another instance of the unforgiving harshness that sometimes characterises rural communities. In the story the widow Ouma Engelbrecht is ostracised by the community because of the incorrect Boer War activities of her son.

These stories are published together here for the first time. Some have appeared before alongside Oom Schalk stories (*Unto Dust*); as selected works (*Selected Stories*); or as miscellanea (*Almost Forgotten Stories*; *Ramoutsa Road*). However, this is the most comprehensive gathering of 'non-Oom Schalk', 'non-Voorkamer' stories by Bosman yet published and they are presented here as a distinct 'third category' in his short story oeuvre – in their own right, rather than as miscellaneous items tucked into the corners of Oom Schalk or Voorkamer collections. Moreover, four of them are published here for the first time ("Jakob's Trek", "The Heart of a Woman", "Night on the Veld" and "The Old Muzzle-loader"); two have never before been collected into volume form ("New Elder" and "Shy Young Man"); and several others are hardly known. "Louis Wassenaar" is the curiosity in the collection: actually the opening of a novel begun in the early 1930s, it is included here especially for the commentary it delivers on how short stories may be devised and interpreted, with a brilliant example included. They are prefaced by a heartfelt essay by Bosman on the state of the South African short story circa 1948 and some commentary on short story writers and writing.

The 'old Transvaal' that Bosman evokes so powerfully in these stories is gone forever. Not only has the name itself disappeared, but the atmosphere of the open veld, of wagons rolling northwards "with spans of Afrikaner oxen like red threaded beads" ("The Old Muzzle-loader"), of neighbours passing the time drinking coffee on the farm stoep, or even of the 'old Johannesburg' with its thriving metropolitan centre and optimistic mining-town bustle, has of course inexorably passed away.

What we have in this collection is a composite portrait of that old Transvaal by a man who knew it intimately, loved it for all of its flaws and quirks, and had the skill to capture its smells and textures in writing. Also discernible in it is a shadowy portrait of the writer himself, reflecting on his practice as a wordsmith with his distinctive wry humour and genial humanistic vision.

My thanks to the Harry Ransom Humanities Research Center at the University of Texas at Austin for allowing me access to its collection and for granting me a British Studies Fellowship for the purpose of researching the Bosman Papers.

Craig MacKenzie
Johannesburg, 2000

The South African Short Story Writer

I N the February, 1948, issue of *Trek* there appeared a review of a book entitled *South African Short Stories*. It was an acid criticism of a collection of short stories garnered by Dr Seary and published by the Cape Town branch of the Oxford University Press. The stories purport to be "representative of South African writers on South African themes." I have read Dr Seary's collection; I also read the review. Edward Davis makes an all too sweeping and condemnatory statement in his summing up in these words: "Dr Seary's anthology is nevertheless as good a selection as possible. No one faced with his task could have done better." This is, of course, an admission by the reviewer that he couldn't have done better himself, but it is also an admission that, in his opinion, the South African writer of short stories is on just about the lowest rung of the literary ladder that it is possible to be. In fact, he might just as well run away and play snakes and ladders.

Of course South Africa, admittedly, has never produced a short story writer within hailing distance of O. Henry (what a wealth of material he would have found in this land of ours for his magic pen!) or a Bret Harte. These men were geniuses in the difficult art of short story writing. Among living short story writers we have no one to compare by a long chalk with America's Steinbeck or Hemingway, or England's Somerset Maugham – one needn't name more. Yet I have read good, clever short stories, few though they may be, by South African writers on South African themes.

Let it be assumed, however, that the reviewer is justified in his damning criticism. At the same time let us probe down to the root of the trouble, see what's the matter and suggest a remedy. Short story writing is one of the most difficult of all literary arts. The technique is not mastered without patience, study and hard work. Writing the average novel is, relatively speaking, an easy matter. The novelist can spread himself (or herself); there can be pages, or even chapters, which are dull – but these can be compensated by the merits of other sections of the book. The canvas is vast. There is no room for such lapses in that miniature, the first-class short story, in which every word must count, every detail must be perfect. Every writer of short stories knows, or should know, of the numerous technical difficulties that must be overcome, the many pitfalls which must be avoided.

Something to remember when weighing up South Africa's achievements in this field is that even in densely populated countries such as Britain and America the novelists outnumber the good short story writers. More writers eventually turn their hand to the novel (the rewards are greater, of course) than to short story writing. The first-rate short story writer is, therefore, a *rara avis*. How many can we expect to find in this country where we have only something over two million Europeans – men, women and children, including imbeciles and gaolbirds?

I do believe, however, that the short story writer in this country can be encouraged to produce something which may eventually make the reviewer and the discerning section of the reading public sit up and take notice. I believe that a very great deal could be done in this sphere by an enterprising publisher (O. U. P. was at least enterprising enough to publish *South African Short Stories*) who would be willing to bring out annually a selection of the best short stories written by living South African writers. I should like to see him get up and announce his intention of producing such a volume in a stentorian voice that could be heard all over South Africa – yea, and beyond her boundaries. I should like him to invite all editors, publishers and surveyors of short stories to submit to him each year a selection of their dozen best short stories. There are many newspapers and periodicals published in this country which I believe would be willing to co-operate. Then I should like to see the publisher offer a prize of £100 (or more) to the writer of the best short story of the year, the author being allowed to retain the copyright. Is that too much to ask in order to encourage the unearthing of a first-class short story writer whose name may be echoed beyond these shores?

What would be the result of such a staggering pronouncement? Why, every discouraged, poorly paid and overworked writer of short stories in the country would say, "What! A hundred quid for a South African short story! The age of miracles is not over! If I don't win that prize this year, I may next." He (or she, be it well understood) would clutch a typewriter or pen and dip it in pathos, bathos, humour, irony, local colour, subtlety, invective, love – yes, even sob-stuff – and he would do his damnedest to produce the very best story of which he was capable. Of course, I know it can be argued that a worthwhile writer should produce the best work he can at all times, regardless of any reward. Quite right. But a writer puts pen to paper in order to earn a living and the time spent upon any given piece of work must bear a reasonable relation to the payment received. A substantial incentive can make him put just that little something more into his work – and oh, how much that little more may mean! (Note: there is a surprising number of first-rate American magazines which frequently pay more than a hundred pounds for a good short story as a matter of course. *Liberty*, for instance, pays between one hundred and five hundred dollars weekly for a short story. That is one reason why the American short story is in every way superior to the average British product.)

If such a prize as I have mentioned were offered, I who have sold a number of short stories in this country (and a few overseas) would dive for my typewriter. At present, I, like other simpletons, sweat, pore, write, re-write, re-type (many times over), curse, and burn the midnight oil, to produce something between 2 000 and 4 000 words in length and mail it off (stamped and addressed envelope enclosed for return of MS. and editor's compliments), to be paid, if it is accepted, at the measly rate of three guineas (or less) a thousand words. And that payment is made 'on publication', which may mean delay of anything up to six months or even more before the princely sum drops into my letter-box.

I have spent a few bob at the races with just as much chance of remuneration (or loss) as writing a short story. A labourer unworthy of his hire earns many times more in the same amount of time as I take to create my brain-child – but with no expenditure of mental, and not much physical, effort. A hack article on something topical churned out in an hour or two will earn the same fee as a short story of the same length. It is one of the minor anomalies of our civilisation. But it is one of the reasons why reviewers can dip their pens in boiling vitriol and spread themselves. There is no encouragement to the short story writer to improve.

You will therefore see, I hope, what an opportunity lies before an enterprising publisher to improve the standard of the short story in this country. It would pay a publisher handsome dividends in the long run to give a fillip to a literary art which has so far received no encouragement in South Africa. In Britain and America there are publications which are entirely devoted to the best stories of the year. Rewards are offered to the writer of the best story. These publications surely cannot prove financial losses otherwise they would not continue to appear year after year. The publisher, after all, is in the business primarily to make money.

South Africa is receiving today more publicity than she has ever had in the past. People are becoming more and more South Africa conscious. The press in England and America devotes a good deal of space to the subject of South Africa. Novels (even poor novels), travel books and articles about this country are finding a more and more ready sale overseas. The short story is lagging far behind and I find it hard to believe that an annual volume (well publicised) of the best short stories written by living writers in South Africa today would not find an equally ready market.

An important point for my enterprising publisher to remember is in the selection of the final, say, twenty to twenty-five stories to be incorporated in the book, which should be worthy and "representative of South African writers on South African themes." The selection should not be the responsibility of one individual but of a panel of at least four persons. These should include a publisher and an editor for, after all, these men read short stories all the year round and have to make a choice of their wares to present to the public. There is no reason why a D. Litt. should not also be included in the selection panel. All stories should be submitted under assumed names. Let there be no favouritism or 'name' to exert undue influence among the members of the panel who, unbiased though they may be, would be only human. We want the best stories, not the best-known names.

Although in the past no encouragement has been given to the short story writer, I feel that he himself is not entirely blameless. How many writers really study the technique of the short story? How many are prepared to devote sufficient sweat and toil to their creations to bring them to perfection?

There are novelists who have secured lasting fame in this country and overseas – Olive Schreiner is probably the most illustrious. South Africa may yet produce a short story writer who may compare not unfavourably with the giants of the past and present. In the meantime I, like many another persevering optimist, will continue, painfully and laboriously, to conceive for two or three guineas a thousand words. Some day I hope to produce a *real* short story. Now what about that publisher of mine doing something about it?

Notes on Short Story Writers

W. W. Jacobs

BECAUSE he has never been in gaol, like O. Henry, or in the gutter, like Edgar Allan Poe, William Wymark Jacobs has been denied much of that artistic glamour that is his due as one of the great masters of a great literary form.

For the world, in spite of its pretence to the contrary, still expects its men of genius to be decorated with sundry wayward splashes; and it gets suspicious when these decorations are missing.

But what is unquestioned is the great and definitive contribution which W. W. Jacobs has made to the art of the short story. His place is as secure as anybody's. As secure as De Maupassant's.

Lots of people have indulged in the interesting but unnecessary pastime of trying to explain what a short story is: they have pointed out that length has got nothing to do with it; that a piece of writing can be as long as you like and still pass as a short story, provided that it conforms to certain technical requirements. W. W. Jacobs talks like that, too. He says all the orthodox text-book things – about a short story being concerned with the exposition of a single theme; that it doesn't deal with developments, and so on. That only shows how innocent W. W. Jacobs is, of course. He is simply trying to explain what other people have said about the form of the short story after reading "The Monkey's Paw."

All I can say, under these circumstances, is that it is very lucky W. W. Jacobs wrote *Many Cargoes* and over 150 stories before he started reading the text-books. In my view a short story is simply a story that doesn't take very long to tell. And there is only one way in which you can tell a story like that. Otherwise the audience walks away.

I believe that W. W. Jacobs has had a very profound influence on the English short story of today. I shall not go into details about this because it is funny how unpleasant lots of people get when you tell them that somebody else has influenced them.

But what is without question is the fact that as recently as fifty years ago there prevailed amongst English writers – even writers of standing – a unique and stately ignorance of what was meant by a short story. W. W. Jacobs told me, once, that I should read these stories – just to see. Instead, I helped myself to some more of his brandy. I gulped it so quick that I coughed. From that he gathered, no doubt, that I had read a fair amount of the stuff he was discussing.

But the English short story of today is different. And W. W. Jacobs has had a lot to do with bringing about this change.

W. W. Jacobs's stock-in-trade is romance. And, as Shakespeare found, a writer doesn't need any more than just that to go on. The most wistful of hopes, the sublimest dreams, the richest and most gaudily arrayed awakenings of triumph and fulfilment – all these have their origin in the human heart.

And it is in his knowledge of human nature that the power of W. W. Jacobs lies. A drunken sailor stumbling out of a pub. A girl tripping down a Wapping pavement, with a fastener in her hat and her heart beating high. Of such is the material of W. W. Jacobs's stories – commonplace characters touched by the magic of the master's hand, to be invested with a sudden charm and a strange and tender dignity. This is W. W. Jacobs's spell. This is the secret of how he weaves his witchery. Bring out your loom and try it.

As a humorist W. W. Jacobs stands high. He tells me that when he and Jerome K. Jerome first came along with their particular brand of humour, there was a certain amount of popular dissatisfaction about it. I can understand that this should have been so with Jerome K. Jerome: there was much of the wild exaggeration and flamboyance of America and Mark Twain in Jerome's treatment of his themes; and English readers did not at first take kindly to this new and tremendous phenomenon of a humour that flung cultures and continents and traditions around, airily.

But it is difficult to understand why W. W. Jacobs got involved, also. Perhaps it was his simplicity that was a trifle bewildering, at first. He seems to write so easily; until you stop and realise what he has done. Then you see the superb and polished artistry in every sentence he has written. The stupendous economy with which his effects are achieved. The deft and cunning touches. The dazzling certainty with which he pulls out the right word, so that it looks as though it just fell like that. And maybe it did.

Latterly, W. W. Jacobs has been wasting a lot of his time puzzling over politics and studying the gold standard. (It is surprising how many humorists go wrong like that.) His politics are not nearly as original as his stories. And I can't judge as to whether or not his ideas on the gold standard are any good. He has written only three stories in the last eight years, he says. I expect that's what comes of reading text-books.

All this is a pity. The world can do with a lot more flashes about the Night Watchman and Bob Pretty; it is about full up with the gold standard dope.

"The Monkey's Paw", which has found its way into practically every short story anthology, is deservedly recognised as one of the world's great stories. Yet I think that Jacobs's other macabre tale, "The Tall House", is as good as "The Monkey's Paw", if not better. W. W. Jacobs tells me that the late President Roosevelt had the same opinion about it: he also said that he preferred "The Tall House." It is pleasing to think that America has had a president who was not only strong on talking hooey to the Middle West, but who was also a discriminating judge of literature.

Nevertheless, what I like best are W. W. Jacobs's love stories. He has put much delicate beauty into them. And I venture to think that these stories will not die easily. I think they will remain when much of what is being written today has been forgotten. That is the way romance has, coming by, disconcertingly, with fragrance and with mockery, luring the children of men from their serious pursuits.

For W. W. Jacobs is, above all, a romantic. He belongs with the dreamers and the singers and the wistful weavers of fairy-tales; when who have gone forth with a high courage and a gay understanding, and when their feet have been unsteady it is because they have walked among the stars.

W. C. Scully

What do you know of the works of W. C. Scully? Ask this question of the average reasonably well-read South African, and you will be amazed at the amount of ignorance that he will reveal.

I had a look at the syllabus for English I, English II and English III at Wits the other day. It's a laugh. It is dominated by contemporary English third-raters of the T. S. Eliot school and class, whose message you haven't got to make any strong cerebral effort to understand, because it's so superficial. And no South African writers. Why do they keep it a secret that we have got classics of our own? I say, without thinking twice about it – if I thought twice I'd probably get so worked up that I would want to start doing violence – that Scully is better than nine-tenths of the *contemporary* English authors whose works are prescribed for the Witwatersrand University courses in English. (I am not talking of the giants of English literature, to whom the world must remain for ever indebted.)

Pauline Smith

It comes almost as a shock to find a South African English writer of the period circa 1925 whose attitude towards South Africa was other than that of an aloof superiority. Perhaps it was not just a matter of chance that of all the writers in this country Pauline Smith, with her *Little Karoo*, has put forth the strongest claim to the perilous and unhappy garland of genius. A love for South Africa would not appear to be an insuperable obstacle in the way of one's becoming a South African writer.

In the early twenties of this century Pauline Smith write a dozen or so stories that were stonily descriptive of Afrikaner life on the Karoo and that were shaped after a fashion that a sculptor would understand with his right hand calloused from the hammer, and that had in them that brooding quality which, in the veld, is poignancy and bitterness and in the hearts of men and women is the waywardness of love. Pauline Smith has also written, among other things, a novel, *The Beadle* But it is a handful of stories, collected in a slender volume and published in the beginning of 1925 under the title *The Little Karoo* that represents this writer's supreme achievement.

As far as I am concerned, she need have written nothing beside these short stories. For there is in them more than a challenge, more than a superb gesture and a direction. They are all charged with a magnificent finality from which one may not withhold the title of greatness.

Anybody can be a writer. You can have anything at all that you want in this world. That is what Christ said. And that is what a professional wrestler told me a couple of days ago. The wrestler said, "Anybody that wants to, if he starts off at it eight o'clock in the morning, will be able to wrestle a bit by the evening." And I say that anybody at all, whether he has an aptitude for it or not, who sits down in the morning to try to write will, by the evening, have become a writer.

I would only like to say that this is not the way in which Pauline Smith became a writer. Her art of writing a short story is closely akin to the art of writing poetry, and when she has delivered her message, she, like the poet Rimbaud, ceased writing. There is no mystery at all about the reasons for which Pauline Smith laid down her pen. It is easy to understand why she stopped writing. "My spinning is all done."

Nearly all of what Pauline Smith has written are love stories. And the lightest love story is laden with frightening things. And Pauline Smith has written her love stories – take "The Sinner" and "The Schoolmaster" as two examples – with a simple intensity that you find in dry, wind-tattered grasses and in poetry.

But before going any further I feel I have to explain something. Pauline Smith knows what she is writing about. She understands the Afrikaner and the veld. Not with the detached understanding of the intellect, which is a brittle thing and betrays you the very moment you start relying on it, but with the warm comprehension of the heart. Pauline Smith's knowledge of her subject is profound and penetrative and strong, passionately so, and her approach is essentially feminine. Her stories are pure with light and very tenderly told and brave. One requires nothing more than this from a woman story-teller. But, also, one demands nothing less.

The result is that there is a wider, more all-embracing truth about life and about the veld that Pauline Smith does not deal with at all. But I want to make clear that for the sake of her art it is right that she cannot see the autumn as melodrama, and that her warm understanding of the spirit of the Afrikaner does not rise to the height of that other love and that further knowing, in which stark tragedy has also got its tinsel side and sorrow is the mask for a carnival.

This wider form of literary creation belongs with the ultimates of art. And it is well that Pauline Smith does not essay this furthest flight of all. She would lay waste her heart if she were to emerge from the high purpose of her inwardness and attempt to depict life in the colours of more starry truth, where a knowledge of humanity comes near to, and therefore is not, mockery.

The strange thing about Pauline Smith's language is that it is more like Afrikaans than English. By this I don't mean that she uses an affected style, or that she overloads her prose with the adventitious introduction of Afrikaans words and phrases, twisting her sentences round to conform to the Afrikaans idiom. It is easy to get a specious sort of local colour this way. For instance, if you want to write a novel about the Middle Ages and you don't know too much about medieval spirit you can achieve a fair degree of success with the judicious use of words like "quotha", "scurvy", "beshrew", "knave", and whatnot. But you have got to be an artist to do it successfully. Lots of people, writing about the backveld, have employed this same trick, in order to get atmosphere. The result is that their stories read like Robert Louis Stevenson's *Black Arrow*.

Pauline Smith's stories are written in an English of a purity to which not even Fowler could object. But there is more than that to her style. Take the last sentence of "The Sinner": "With stupid, fumbling fingers, and eyes made redder than ever with tears, he tied his bundles together and took the road to Platkops dorp." As for me, more than once, reading her stories – particularly "The Sisters" – I was brought to realise, with something almost like a start, that the page in front of me was printed, not in Afrikaans, but in English.

Pauline Smith's stories are already for ever a part of South African literature. They depict South African life with a truth and a beauty which no writer has so far achieved in the short story form written in Afrikaans.

Preface to *Veld-trails and Pavements*

T HIS volume is designed by the publishers to reflect the main trends in the development of the South African short story in English. The selections have been made from stories that have been written over a period of approximately three-quarters of a century; that is, from the work of the first exponents of the art of the short story in this country to that of our younger writers of today. While it cannot be expected that the list of contents will meet with unanimous approval, we nevertheless believe that, making due allowance for individual differences in taste and judgement, the stories we have selected are representative of the best that South African literature offers in this genre.

The short story, as we understand it today, is for all practical purposes a new form of literary art. In one sense, of course, the story is as old as literature. Folklore is made up of short stories. The Egyptian Book of the Dead and the Bible are full of short stories. Then there are works as divergent as *The Arabian Nights*, Cervantes's *Contes*, the *Gesta Romanorum*, *The Decameron*. Indeed, when we come to examine the treasures of world literature, it almost seems as though our problem is to escape from the short story: what seems hard is to find something that is *not* a short story. In the same way, the life of each human being, from the cradle to the grave, is made up of a series of short stories.

The modern short story accepts all the foregoing premises and subscribes to their implications: no form of art can exist that is not close to life. But in the hands of the great writers of the last few generations that short story has become moulded into a definite, clearly recognisable shape.

The greatest single contribution to the development of the short story was made by the American writers of the last century, Edgar Allan Poe lighting the way for Bret Harte and Ambrose Bierce and O. Henry. With tales like "The Fall of the House of Usher", "William Wilson", "Lygeia", "Berenice" and – in a different category – "Marie Roget" and "The Cask of Amontillado", Edgar Allan Poe originated what writers of the succeeding decades slowly came to recognise as a new form of literary art, holding out fascinating possibilities for innovation in respect of both subject matter and treatment. Half a century after Edgar Allan Poe, Brander Matthews in his "Philosophy of the Short Story" formulated certain important technical principles, based on his classic differentiation between the short-story (which he hyphenated thus) and a story which is merely short.

Edgar Allan Poe, who was himself heavily indebted to the German romantic Gothicists, exercised a powerful influence on the French writers of the later nineteenth century. Poe inspired not only the French poets Baudelaire, Verlaine and Rimbaud, but also the French short story writers, including Mérimée, Daudet and De Maupassant. Anton Chekhov, through his almost obsessional concentration on a single aspect of character, imparted to the short story a direction which, although powerful, was to become identified in the following generation with some of the less admirable features of literary effort, a photographic 'realism' being frequently made to serve as a substitute for creative originality.

South African English writing is at the present moment passing through an interesting stage in its development from a 'colonial' literature into a nationally conscious art. In prose – and more especially through the medium of the short story – we are beginning to witness the rise of an authentically South African school of letters. The South African short story offers scope for great and original literary expression. It is, above all else, incumbent on our writers to remain true to their own environment and traditions.

Jakob's Trek

For a whole week, slowly and with great difficulty, they journeyed. At intervals there were indications of wagons having passed that way. But those patches of trampled grass and bush could scarcely be termed a road. Jolting, the wagon rolled onward. When the long, turning spokes of the wheels did indeed come to a rest, there was a voice shouting, "Blokland! Platkop!" – followed by the dull shuffling of hooves as the wagon went lumbering on through the thin shadows of the thorn-trees. The hot hoops of the wagon wheels would pass over a sandy stretch with a sound as of sighing, which would grow muted again as the grass scorched to whiteness.

His broad shoulders stooping slightly, Jakob de Jager walked beside the hind oxen, swinging the whip whose thongs had more than once been spliced. He thrust back his hat to wipe the sweat from his forehead. "Lord," he said, "this heat."

During the past week this had been going on. The sun rose in the morning, white and glowing in the east, and went on its monotonous journey through a cloudless sky. Then in the evening there would come a cool breath only when the sky behind the bushes changed to a tawny yellow, deepening finally to a swart scarlet. A week's journey now separated them from their own people, who lived in the area about Winburg, dwelling comparatively close together. Their farms were large and the roads unlovely.

Jakob had decided to trek on further. On the night before their leave-taking his wife's father had read to them out of the Bible slowly and with solemnity and had then offered up a prayer for them with much earnestness. Next morning, with the first pale gleams lighting the hills, he had assisted Hanna and the two children aboard the wagon. They trekked away into the fresh dawning of a new day. Jakkals, the coloured man, led the oxen. His wife, Sabiena, sat on the wagon with a child in her arms.

There was a spruit where, the wagon fast in the mud, they struggled for the better part of a day in the heat of the sun. But they won through. Jakob knew what he wanted. Had he not once, in the company of some other Boers, visited these parts on horseback? And when, in the afternoon, they had dismounted on an eminence, and he had watched the shining breadth of the Vaal River flowing away beneath the setting sun, there had awakened in him a yearning to settle by the banks of that great river. To build a house, maybe, there in one of the ravines that edged away blue and cool from the Vaal.

Virginal the world was here, hushed and untroubled. In the evening he had lain a long while, listening to the serene sounds of the river in its flow by dark trees into an unknown world, spread wide under burning stars. Because that memory had remained with him, he was now trekking through these parts to find for himself a place of abode along the banks of that mighty stream.

He had been journeying for days, now. Sometimes it seemed to him that what he had embarked on was a piece of folly. . . flinging away the contentment that the society of one's fellow man brings one, for this life that held out prospects only of hardship and grim toil. And then of a sudden the oppressive heat became easier to bear; his rising doubts vanished. Across the silence of the high noon there came to him the sound of a deep murmuring. For a moment it might almost have been the wind in a poplar grove, troubling the stillness with a sound like running water. Jakob cracked the whip with new energy. The oxen seemed to become imbued with an animation, suddenly, now that they were approaching the river. At the foot of a hill the trek came to a halt. Here in front of them was the Vaal. Gleaming through the bush, it slid away in long wrinkles or splashed down between smooth rocks to flow on quietly again in the indigenous shade of overhanging branches.

"Look, Hanna," he said, peering in through the flap of the wagon-tent. "Look, here is the river I told you about. Look, children, is it not a fine stretch of water? We'll have no worries here about getting drinking water for the cattle. There is even land here that we can till." And he pointed to the level stretches bordering the river.

Through the opening in the wagon-tent, Hanna glanced listlessly at the river. She was very tired and the heat inside the wagon had made her irritable. It was not easy for her to evince much enthusiasm at the sight of the river. That place in which her people had remained behind represented security to her, and when she thought of her children, it was that security that she desired most. In times of illness there would be nobody knowledgeable at hand to aid and advise her. Here she would be cut off from everything. They would have to start from scratch.

"Old girl," Jakob said, speaking as though he had to justify himself – for the sight of that broad stretch of water had awakened no happiness in his wife's gaze – "You know, where there is water one can do a lot. We'll prosper here. Just look at that kloof. We'll settle down very comfortably here."

"That is well," Hanna said, resignedly. "But you must hurry, so that we can outspan. Look where the sun is."

Somewhat dejected, he went back to the oxen. It was obvious that his wife did not view things in the light he did. If he failed here, she would take it ill. In the trek up from the Cape she had suffered much. They had lost three children. She was keen on remaining near her people in Winburg. She wanted some measure of company. She wanted people to turn to in time of need. On the other hand, what he wanted was a large farm, and he wanted to work it up from the bare veld. He was content here. In these surroundings he could feel at home for the rest of his life.

Once more the oxen strained at the wagon. The wagon went lumbering on. "Turn away just beyond that thorn-tree," Jakob called out to Jakkals. "And then go on to the foot of the mountain."

It was harder going than ever, now, winding in and out between the thorn-trees, floundering across ditches; the wheels bumping over tussock sods. At long last Jakob's welcome shout, "Hook-han-o-o", came to disturb the age-old quiet of the veld. And the wagon-spokes ceased their turning. And the shadow of the wagon lay long and dark athwart the patch of grass between the thorn-trees.

Higher up, hidden in the long grass and about it the tracks of wild animals, was a spring. Yokes were lifted from tired humps. The oxen stared about them in a vacant way and then began moving off in the direction of the water. Hanna and the children alighted from the wagon. Presently each was engaged in helping to prepare for the coming night. The broad shadow of the mountain fell cool and deep across their activities, for back of the mountain the sun had already disappeared. In the distance, strips of yellow sunlight still lit up the way along which they had journeyed. When these gleams, too, went, Hanna felt chill and strange at the foot of the lonely mountain.

"Do make us a fire, Jakob," she said. She folded her arms and shivered. Jakkals brought firewood. Tongues of flame shot up swiftly through the crackling wood. . . the only radiance in an evening world, sombre with twilight. Jakkals methodically skinned a small steenbok that Jakob had shot earlier in the day. He folded up the supple skin and then went to wash his bloodstained hands at the river. Presently the fragrance of roast meat filled the air. Shadows flitted about the fire. Supper over, the little group gathered peacefully around the fire. The light flickered over them and flowed away into the caves of the dark among the trees beyond. "What do you think of it here, Jakkals?" Jakob asked, his tone cheerless. For he knew what made his wife so subdued. He knew her nostalgia; he understood about her longing for a life that held more comfort.

"I can't say, master," Jakkals answered. "These parts frighten me. I like the open veld. But I feel as though I am being stalked by these trees. At any moment I sort of expect something to pounce on to me from behind, out of the dark. But, of course, master, there is plenty of water here. That's one thing we won't have to worry about."

Japie, the son, sat next to his father. He gazed into the dark, on his thin, tired face a look of expectancy. He was a quiet child. He had heard many stories of wild animals, told him by Jakkals. He now expected to see fiery eyes approaching out of a darkness that held much of mystery and terror. Japie was fifteen. He had learnt a good deal while on trek with his parents, and could make himself useful. The twelve-year-old daughter, Malie, sat leaning against her mother. Malie's hair hung down her shoulders in two thin pigtails. Her eyes were large and blue. She had her father's looks. They sat by the fire for a long while – father and son, mother and daughter.

Jakob knew this sort of life. He had seen his father embark on the same struggle three times in succession – starting with bare veld and making to arise from it, in the face of a stubborn nature, the orderliness of a farm. That was in the Cape. Jakob recalled in melancholy the white homesteads and the oak-trees and the lamp-light gleaming on old furniture. His father had trained his children in the habits of industry. And not with friendly words, but with thrashings that they would remember to the end of their lives. His one concern was to force his children to realise that life was a stern and remorseless struggle, in which there was no place for a weakling or a coward, who would be only a burden to himself and others.

His parents lay buried in the Free State. They had taken part in the Great Trek and had set about, for the last time, working up a new farm in the Winburg area. Jakob's father had been a man of tremendous physical strength. His sons had inherited his strength. Furthermore, his father could not remain settled in one place for long. The moment things were running smoothly, he would be overtaken by a restless urge. He would be sullen for days. He would insist on the need for leaving the old farm and making a fresh start on a new piece of land. In the beginning, Jakob's mother had protested. But afterwards she grew resigned to these constant changes, accepting with a sigh her husband's demand that they should trek once more.

And now. . . here was Jakob himself sitting on the veld with his wife and children. He, too, had the trek-lust.

"Hanna," he asked, suddenly tender and sympathetic, "are you very tired? It's about time we got some rest."

His wife was no doubt thinking of the three children that they had lost, each dying so soon after the other. As the aftermath to her bitter weeping, then, she was left with the affliction of severe headaches.

"Yes, Jakob," she answered, gazing intently into the fire, "we've passed through a difficult time. And it was very hot today. My head is aching dreadfully again. But I expect we'll all feel better tomorrow."

He looked at her, seeking to penetrate her thoughts.

"We'll be happy here, Hanna," he said again, as though trying to convince her. "We'll do well here, and there will be nobody to worry us."

She went on staring into the fire, and did not answer. Then she covered her eyes with her hand. Jakob stood up. He went to see whether Jakkals had rounded up the oxen, which had to be tethered for the night. When he got beyond the circle of light he stood still, listening to the sounds the river made as it flowed away peacefully under the stars.

It was good, here. Here he wanted to stay for a long, a very long time.

A Tale Writ in Water

THE story of the Tsamma pool is a story of the northwest Cape; of that part of the Cape Province which has perhaps not known European settlement for quite as long as the Western Province has done. Nevertheless, whitewashed farmhouses with their old-fashioned abba chimneys have been dotted over an extensive coastal strip in that area since before the middle of the eighteenth century. And we know that in the 1780s there was in these parts a drostdy as far away from Cape Town as Plettenberg Bay.

This is a pleasant land, between the mountains and the sea, and in the wooded parts there are many pools like the one to which this story relates. Ringed with mighty assegai trees and yellow-woods and the occasional stinkwood, the water in such a pool is of an intense blue when seen from above. But when you come closer, approaching to the water's edge through the tall trees and picking your way over the rounded stones like a cobbled pathway, you realise that the water in these pools is of a golden-brown colour – almost the shade of Nagmaal wine.

This story of the Tsamma pool is one that I have only heard tell; and I never knew the people in it – the people in the story or the people in the pool. And when I have got to the end of this story – which has been told to me a number of times, it being of a legendary nature – you will realise that it is not a story of anything that could really have happened. But that doesn't mean that it might not be a true story.

A legend is like that. . .

Mythical or otherwise, it is a pretty story. And I still think that it has as much authenticity as any story that gets told on a winter's evening before a fire in the voorkamer, when the person who is telling the story actually knew the people in it (or so he says); although towards the end of the story, when the peach brandy has gone the rounds a couple of times, the storyteller might perhaps forget, for a little while, just which people were in the story and which were in the pool.

As for this present tale, well, the central character in it is that rock pool, set in the midst of the tall trees. And although the two young lovers, Annie Brink and Zacharias Welthagen, come into this story right enough, they enter it almost timidly, and their visit is brief, fleeting.

And their only means of gaining access to this story is through a little wooden gate which at one time stood near the edge of the pool.

Now, geologists hold the theory that this rock pool, which the natives and white farmers in the neighbourhood call the Tsamma pool, was many thousands of years ago an appendage of a nearby river, which burst its banks in a flood season, inundating a wide area. But if that were so, it must be that the pool has since become like one of the yellow-woods lining its edge, and that it has thrust its own dark roots twisting into the earth. For in times of drought the level of the Tsamma pool has been lowered hardly at all. And there is a tradition that the pool remained full once, long ago, when the river had ceased to flow.

That must have been a fearful time of drought. I have come across one or two old people living in these parts who place it in the time of their grandfathers – that year in which there was no water in the river. I can imagine what that dry river-bed would have looked like, with scattered boulders and with the sun-dried hoof-prints of cattle and of a few shy springbok and blesbok. There might even have been the footprints of a Bushman. And you would have discovered that the Bushman was just about as shy as the blesbok, if you had measured with your eye the distance his legs were stretched when he went bounding along the river-bed. The percussion cap was beginning to replace the flintlock in the Boers' muzzle-loaders, just about then, this causing the Bushman to lengthen his stride appreciably.

I like the idea of that little wooden gate at the edge of the pool.

Naturally, I have heard more than one version of this story of the Tsamma pool, but in each version there is that little wooden gate that was almost all that remained of a fence that many years before had enclosed the grounds of a large house. It was believed that this house had been built by the old Hollanders.

The foundations of the house and part of a high stoep were still there when Annie Brink and Zacharias Welthagen came into this story, walking hand in hand. The springbok and the blesbok and the Bushman had gone.

What was most singular about the Tsamma pool was the fact that its blue waters sometimes reflected clouds other than those floating lazily overhead; and mirrored trees other than those standing on the banks. That was how the pool got its name, from a native word meaning to remember. When a stranger first learns some of these details, it sometimes seems queer to him that the natives should have given the pool a name whose meaning is connected with 'remembering', when they should rather have called it by a name signifying 'to forget.' Later on, however, the stranger begins to realise that the pool bears its correct descriptive appellation, after all.

The spring would have come and gone and the summer would be well advanced, with the trees on the edge of the water clothed in rich green – and the Tsamma pool would still reflect the gaunt trunks and naked branches of the trees as they stood in mid-winter. The Tsamma pool would practise this deception only on certain occasions, mostly in the heat of summer and at high noon.

The natives said that the mystery of the pool was in some way connected with the affairs of their ancestral spirits, and the Boers in the neighbourhood were inclined to accept this view, in spite of the explanations that a schoolmaster there had once tried to give of what he called an ordinary manifestation of the laws of nature.

The schoolmaster said that the water at the edge of the pool appeared only through an optical illusion at times to reflect objects other than those on the bank. This was by no means a unique phenomenon, but could be compared with the visionary appearance of lakes and trees in arid deserts, and was due to the light waves being diverted from their straight path through the expansion of the atmosphere. The schoolmaster drew curved lines on a piece of paper and wrote on it expressions like "lowest layer of air" to show what he meant.

What the schoolmaster said did not sound altogether unreasonable. But his explanation was rejected by the local inhabitants when, on a later occasion, he had tried to tell a man who had seen a ghost that this was also just a fallacy of vision, caused by variations in the refractive index of the atmosphere after sunset. The Boers knew enough about ghosts to know that there was a lot more to a ghost than just that.

The result of all this has been that it is contended – today, even – that the pool, on occasion, reflects winter trees in summer, the reason for this being that the pool still remembers the previous winter. (Incidentally, nobody seems to have thought of suggesting that all this might be due to *forgetfulness* on the part of the pool, mindless of the passage of the seasons, forgetting to fit itself to the demands of a new summertime.)

And it is arising out of the above-mentioned belief, no doubt, that the story has gained currency of there having been a day when the Tsamma pool remembered other things besides last winter's trees. A mingling of various elements of reality and superstition forms, I suppose, the material out of which all legends are created.

It was on a hot summer's day, with the Tsamma pool again remembering the past (and very vividly, too, judging by how bare were the branches that it reflected), when Annie Brink and Zacharias Welthagen came through that little white gate, walking hand in hand.

Moreover, it seemed as though the pool was recalling not merely the last winter, but a winter of many years ago. For, according to the legend, when Annie and Zacharias came to the edge of the pool, and looked into the water, a very strange sight greeted their gaze. Below them, reflected in the water, they saw, indeed, a young and good-looking couple. They recognised themselves easily enough, in spite of the fact that the young man in the water had curled side-whiskers, while Zacharias Welthagen was clean-shaven; and in spite of the fact that the girl holding the hand of the young man with the whiskers had two black spots on her brightly painted cheeks that dimpled on the moving water – while Annie's face was not made up at all.

But it was clear, from the way in which the couple imaged in the water were dressed, that the pool was remembering some time of long ago. For the girl wore a grand frock of rose-coloured satin, and her straw hat had a wide, sweeping brim and flowers, while the young man's suit was of a rich velvet, and he wore white lace at his cuffs. This was in startling contrast to Annie Brink's cheap print dress and cotton kappie – not even to mention Zacharias Welthagen's patched trousers and veldskoens that were an antithesis to seemliness.

Zacharias professed amusement at the elegance of the youth and maiden rippling in warm colours on the surface of the water. Annie, her gaze on the flowers on the girl's hat, breathed a deep sigh. The next moment Zacharias drew her to him, and the wind, stirring through the trees, blew a strand of Annie's dark hair against her lover's cheek. The images in the water patterned themselves after their prototypes on land; and the same wind ruffled, very gently, the surface of the pool and the two reflected figures standing, in velvet and satin, with their arms about each other.

Annie Brink and Zacharias Welthagen went to the pool again several times after that, at the same hour of the day. And each time they met once more their gaudy shadows in the pool.

Then, one day, Annie Brink and Zacharias Welthagen again came through that little gate, and walked hand in hand to the edge of the pool; they looked in. And at what they saw then Annie Brink wept bitterly. For the girl in the satin frock and the wide-brimmed hat stood there alone.

The Affair at Ysterspruit

IT was in the Second Boer War, at the skirmish of Ysterspruit, near Klerksdorp, in February, 1902, that Johannes Engelbrecht, eldest son of Ouma Engelbrecht, widow, received a considerable number of bullet wounds, from which he subsequently died. And when she spoke about the death of her son in battle, Ouma Engelbrecht dwelt heavily on the fact that Johannes had fought bravely. She would enumerate his wounds, and, if you were interested, she would trace in detail the direction that each bullet took through the body of her son.

If you liked stories of the past, and led her on, Ouma Engelbrecht would also mention, after a while, that she had a photograph of Johannes in her bedroom. It was with great difficulty that a stranger could get her to bring out that photograph. But she usually showed it, in the end. And then she would talk very fast about people not being able to understand the feelings that went on in a mother's heart.

"People put the photograph away from them," she would say, "and they turn it face downwards on the rusbank. And all the time I say to them, no, Johannes died bravely. I say to them that they don't know how a mother feels. One bullet came in from in front, just to the right of his heart, and it went through his gall bladder and then struck a bone in his spine and passed out through his hip. And another bullet. . . "

So she would go on while the stranger studied the photograph of her son Johannes, who died of wounds received in the skirmish at Ysterspruit.

When the talk came round to the old days, leading up to and including the Second Boer War, I was always interested when they had a photograph that I could examine, at some farmhouse in that part of the Groot Marico District that faces towards the Kalahari. And when they showed me, hanging framed against a wall of the voorkamer – or having brought it from an adjoining room – a photograph of a burgher of the South African Republic, father or son or husband or lover, then it was always with a thrill of pride in my land and my people that I looked on a likeness of a hero of the Boer War.

I would be equally interested whether it were the portrait of a bearded kommandant or of a youngster of fifteen. Or of a newly appointed veldkornet, looking important, seated on a riempiestoel with his Mauser held upright so that it would come into the photograph, but also turned slightly to the side, for fear that the muzzle should cover up part of the veldkornet's face, or a piece of his manly chest. And I would think that that veldkornet never sat so stiffly on his horse – certainly not on the morning when the commando set out for the Natal border. And he would have looked less important, although perhaps more solemn, on a night when the empty bully-beef tins rattled against the barbed wire in front of a blockhouse, and the English Lee-Metfords spat flame.

I was a school-teacher, many years ago, at a little school in the Marico Bushveld, near the border of the Bechuanaland Protectorate. The Transvaal Education Department expected me to visit the parents of the schoolchildren in the area at intervals. But even if this huisbesoek were not part of my after-school duties, I would have gone and visited the parents in any case. And when I discovered, after one or two casual calls, that the older parents were a fund of first-class story material, that they could hold the listener enthralled with tales of the past, with embroidered reminiscences of Transvaal life in the old days, then I became very conscientious about huisbesoek.

"What happened after that, Oom?" I would say, calling on a parent for about the third week in succession, "when you were trekking through the kloof that night, I mean, and you had muzzled both the black calf with the dappled belly and your daughter, so that Mojaja's men would not be able to hear anything?"

And then the oom would knock out the ash from his pipe on to his veldskoen and he would proceed to relate – his words a slow and steady rumble and with the red dust of the road in their sound, almost – a tale of terror or of high romance or of soft laughter.

It was quite by accident that I came across Ouma Engelbrecht in a two-roomed, mud-walled dwelling some little distance off the Government Road and a few hundred yards away from the homestead of her son-in-law, Stoffel Brink, on whom I had called earlier in the afternoon. I had not been in the Marico very long, then, and my interview with Stoffel Brink had been, on the whole, unsatisfactory. I wanted to know how deep the Boer trenches were dug into the foot of the koppies at Magersfontein, where Stoffel Brink had fought. Stoffel Brink, on the other hand, was anxious to learn whether, in regard to what I taught the children, I would follow the guidance of the local school committee, of which he was chairman, or whether I was one of that new kind of school-teacher who went by a little printed book of subjects supplied by the Education Department. He added that this latter class of school-master was causing a lot of unpleasantness in the Bushveld through teaching the children that the earth moved round the sun, and through broaching similar questions of a political nature.

I replied evasively, with the result that Stoffel Brink launched forth for almost an hour on the merits of the old-fashioned Hollander school-master, who could teach the children all he knew himself in eighteen months, because he taught them only facts.

"If a child stays at school longer than that," Stoffel Brink added, "then the rest of the time he can only learn lies."

I left about then, and on my way back, a little distance from the road and half concealed by tall bush, I found the two-roomed dwelling of Ouma Engelbrecht.

It was good, there.

I could see that Ouma Engelbrecht did not have much time for her son-in-law, Stoffel Brink. For when I mentioned his references to education, when I had merely sought to learn some details about the Boer trenches at Magersfontein, she said that maybe he could learn all there was to know in eighteen months, but he had not learnt how to be ordinarily courteous to a stranger who came to his door – a stranger, more-over, who was a schoolmaster asking information about the Boer War.

Then, of course, she spoke about her son, Johannes, who didn't have to hide in a Magersfontein trench, but who was sitting straight up on his horse when all those bullets went through him at Ysterspruit, and who died of his wounds some time later. Johannes had always been such a well-behaved boy, Ouma Engelbrecht told me, and he was gentle and kind-hearted.

She told me many stories of his childhood and early youth. She spoke about a time when the span of red Afrikaner oxen got stuck with the wagon in the drift, and her husband and the labourers, with long whip and short sjambok, could not move them – and then Johannes had come along and he had spoken softly to the red Afrikaner oxen, and he had called on each of them by name, and the team had made one last mighty effort, and had pulled the wagon through to the other side.

"And yet they never understood him in these parts," Ouma Engelbrecht continued. "They say things about him, and I hardly ever talk of him any more. And when I show them his portrait, they hardly even look at it, and they put the picture away from them, and when they are sitting on that rusbank where you are sitting now, they place the portrait of Johannes face downwards beside them."

I told Ouma Engelbrecht, laughing reassuringly the while, that I stood above the pettiness of local intrigue. I told her that I had already noticed that there were all kinds of queer undercurrents below the placid surface of life in the Groot Marico. There was the example of what had happened that very afternoon, when her son-in-law, Stoffel Brink, had conceived a nameless prejudice against me, simply because I was not prepared to teach the schoolchildren that the earth was flat. I told her that it was ridiculous to imagine that a man in my position, a man of education and wide tolerance, should allow himself to be influenced by local Dwarsberge gossip.

Ouma Engelbrecht spoke freely, then, and the fight at Ysterspruit lived for me again – Kemp and De la Rey and the captured English convoy, the ambush and the booty of a million rounds of ammunition. It was almost as though the affair at Ysterspruit was being related to me, not by a lonely woman whose son received his death wounds on the vlaktes near Klerksdorp, but by a burgher who had taken a prominent part in the battle.

And so, naturally, I wanted to see the photograph of her son, Johannes Engelbrecht.

When it came to the Boer War (although I did not say that to Ouma Engelbrecht), I didn't care if a Boer commander was not very competent or very cunning in his strategy, or if a burgher was not particularly brave. It was enough for me that he had fought. And to me General Snyman, for instance, in spite of the history books' somewhat unflattering assessment of his military qualities, was a hero, none the less. I had seen General Snyman's photograph, somewhere: that face that was like Transvaal blouklip; those eyes that had no fire in them, but a stubborn and elemental strength. You still see Boers in the backveld with that look today.

In my mind I had contrasted the portraits of General Snyman and Comte de Villebois Mareuil, the Frenchman who had come all the way from Europe to shoulder a Mauser for the Transvaal Republic. De Villebois, poet and romantic, last-ditch champion of the forlorn hope and the heroic cause. . . Oh, they were very different, these two men, De Villebois Mareuil, the French nobleman, and Snyman, the Boer. But I had an equal admiration for them both.

Anyway, it was well on towards evening when Ouma Engelbrecht, yielding at last to my cajoleries and entreaties, got up slowly from her chair and went into the adjoining room. She returned with a photograph enclosed in a heavy black frame. I waited, tense with curiosity, to see the portrait of that son of hers who had died of wounds at Ysterspruit, and whose reputation the loose prattle of the neighbourhood had invested with a dishonour as dark as the frame about his photograph.

Flicking a few specks of dust from the portrait, Ouma Engelbrecht handed over the picture to me.

And she was still talking about the things that went on in a mother's heart, things of pride and sorrow that the world did not understand, when, in an unconscious reaction, hardly aware of what I was doing, I placed beside me on the rusbank, face downwards, the photograph of a young man whose hat brim was cocked on the right side, jauntily, and whose jacket with narrow lapels was buttoned up high. With a queer jumble of inarticulate feelings I realised that, in the affair at Ysterspruit, they were all Mauser bullets that had passed through the youthful body of Johannes Engelbrecht, National Scout.

A Boer Rip van Winkel

E VERY writer has got, lying around somewhere in a suitcase or a
trunk, various parts of a story that he has worked on from time to
time and that he has never finished, because he hasn't been able
to find out how the theme should be handled. Such a story – that I have
had lying in a suitcase for many years – centres around the things that
happened to Herklaas van Wyk.

The plot of a story has no particular appeal for me. I feel that to sit
down and work out a plot does not call for the highest form of literary
inspiration. Rather does that form of activity recall the skill of the in-
ventor.

My own stories that I like best are those that have just grown. Some
mood, conjured up in half a dozen words, has set me going, and it has
often happened to me that only when I have got to very near the end in
the writing of it, has the shape of the story suddenly dawned on me.
And more than once I have been surprised to find what a very old tale
it was that has kept me from the chimney corner. Agreeably surprised,
that is, for I have a preference for old tales.

But my inability to finish writing the story of Herklaas van Wyk is
not due to the denouement not having taken some recognisable form in
my mind within the last few hundred words. It hasn't been that kind of
writer's problem: I didn't put my hand in the hat and a story came out
that wouldn't unfold. On the contrary, this story told itself quite all
right, in all its main essentials. What is more, within the first few para-
graphs I realised very clearly to what general class of story it belonged.
But there were so many hiatuses between the time when Herklaas van
Wyk was last seen with the remnants of the Losberg commando, towards the end of the Boer War, in 1902, and the time when he was captured with General Kemp outside Upington in the rebellion of 1914.

If I could fill in that interval of a dozen years satisfactorily, I would
still be able to write the story of Herklaas van Wyk. Yet the very fascination of this story is intimately bound up with the *nature* of that lacu-
na. It is no new thing to have a story of which the end is a mystery –
something that the reader must work out for himself with or without a
clue supplied by the author. But when the middle part of a story – which
gives the atmosphere to the whole sequence of real and imaginary
events – is missing, then I feel that I am confronted with an artistic

44

problem of an order that I am not sure it is wise for a writer to tackle.

I don't mind writing a story in which the plot is vague. But when the atmosphere isn't there – the background and the psychology and the interplay of situation and character – then what is left isn't my idea of a story.

The events with which Herklaas van Wyk was connected in the early part of 1902 were commonplace enough. There are still a number of Boers alive today who were on commando with him. Kritzinger's invasion of the Cape Colony is an episode that has passed into history. And a considerable body of Boers, members of commandos that kept being split up into ever-smaller groups, succeeded in penetrating to the Atlantic Ocean and in remaining in the field, deep inside the Cape Colony, long after the main commando had retreated beyond the Vaal.

It was in 1902 that Herklaas van Wyk, then promoted to the rank of veldkornet, caught sight, in the blue distance, of the unquiet Atlantic. The small body of men pushed on to the beach. They had come a long way, from the Transvaal and the Free State, and also from the Karoo, where a number of Cape rebels had joined the fighting forces of the Republics. It was a mixed group of burghers that came to a halt on the white sand of the beach south of Okiep.

Herklaas van Wyk rode his horse along the shore for a considerable distance. The burghers galloped on behind their veldkornet, the hooves of their horses kicking up a spray of damp sea-sand. For they rode along that strip of beach from which the waves had withdrawn in the ebbing of the Atlantic.

Eventually Herklaas van Wyk reined in his horse. His hand shielding his eyes, he gazed for a long while at the place where the sea and sky met on the horizon. He had known two years before that the Boer War was lost for the Transvaal and the Free State. One last hope had returned to him, early that morning, when he had caught sight of the ocean. That hope, too, had vanished now. He realised that he would not be able, with the handful of burghers under his command, to invade England.

Facing out to the sea, Herklaas van Wyk slowly took off his hat.

"It's no good, kêrels," he called out above the roar of the waves and the wind, "we'll have to go back again. There's no drift around here where we'll be able to get our horses through."

About Herklaas van Wyk there was a certain measure of grandeur even in defeat.

And his story, up to that time when the sea-wind was whistling through his black beard, was straightforward enough. In fact, you can read about him in any history book dealing with that period. But it is on his way back to the Transvaal, when he and his men had to elude flying English columns and had to cross barbed-wire fences with blockhouses threaded on to them, that Herklaas van Wyk quits the pages of printed history, complete with dates and place-names, and enters the realm of legend.

It is generally accepted that he was still in the field when the Boer War ended in May, 1902. His own story is that he crept into a deserted rondavel at the foot of a koppie in the Upington District, and that he fell asleep there, with his Mauser beside him, and his horse tethered to a thorn-tree.

Another story – subscribed to on doubtful authority by fellow members of the rebel commando that surrendered with Herklaas van Wyk in 1915, after General Kemp had failed to take Upington – seeks to account for that interval of a dozen years in a different fashion. In terms of this latter attempt at reconstructing the facts, all that happened to Herklaas van Wyk between 1902, the end of the Boer War, and 1914, the year of the outbreak of the rebellion, was that he lived on some farm in the Upington District as a bywoner. It is readily conceivable, protagonists of this standpoint declare, that he slept quite a lot during that period, especially on hot afternoons when his employer had sent him out to look for strayed cattle. Who has not heard – this school of the doubters asks – of a bywoner lying asleep in his rondavel when he should be at the borehole pumping water?

I can only reply that this theory which represents him as a decadent bywoner does not fit in with my conception of Herklaas van Wyk as a person.

A third school of theorists, drawing attention to the scar of an old bullet wound that Herklaas van Wyk still carried above his left temple when he rode with Kemp in 1915, offers another explanation of that interim period. Quite likely that bullet, searing the flesh at the side of his head, caused loss of memory, they say. Quite likely Herklaas van Wyk did become a bywoner when the Boer War ended. And then, in 1914, when he again heard the hoof-beats of commandos coming out of the veld, and the rattling of musketry, the past was suddenly brought back to him, and he was once more in the saddle, with his Mauser and bandolier. The Boer War came back to him in a single rush. Only, the bywoner period now sank into oblivion. Memory does play tricks like that.

Well, I must confess that I don't care particularly for this latter theory, either.

I still prefer Herklaas van Wyk's own story, which he told to anybody who would listen, after he had been captured by Botha's Government forces. For one thing, if we accept Herklaas van Wyk's account of his long sleep in the abandoned rondavel at the foot of a koppie in the Upington District, we have the material for a South African legend as stirring as the one that Washington Irving chronicled. Van Wyk and Van Winkel. This is surely no idle coincidence. Above all, there is a Gothic quality in Herklaas van Wyk's own story – a gloomy magnificence that is never absent from the interior of a rondavel at the foot of a koppie, if that koppie is composed of ironstone.

Herklaas van Wyk asleep in a dark corner, waiting, a backveld Barbarossa, for his far-off awakening, in an hour filled with the thunder of horse-hooves and the noise of battle.

The old man with the white beard and the rusty Mauser and the walking skeleton of a horse had been with Kemp's rebel commando for the best part of a week of dispirited running away from the Government forces. It now began to dawn on the little band of 1914 rebels that Oom Herklaas van Wyk was (as they interpreted it) in his second childhood. It was clear that he thought the year was 1902; it was obvious that he did not know that he was a rebel who had taken the field against the Union troops; instead, he spoke of himself as a Transvaal burgher, and he referred to Cronje's surrender at Paardeberg, scornfully, as though it had taken place yesterday.

He was very puzzled, also, when he learnt for the first time that the rebel commando was being pursued by a column of Botha-men.

"But if Botha is chasing us," Herklaas van Wyk demanded, "who is fighting Kitchener?"

Thus it came about, one evening when the rebels were encamped in a bluegum plantation on the road to Upington, that a lot of explanations were made.

"I remember the day you joined us, Oom Herklaas," Jan Gouws, a young rebel, said after Herklaas van Wyk had told his story and they had persuaded him that the year was, indeed, 1915, and that he was not now fighting in the Boer War. "Your white beard was blowing in the

47

wind, Oom Herklaas, and several of us laughed at the awkward way your old horse cantered, throwing his legs all to one side. So you really say you slept for twelve years?"

"I believe now – now that you've told me," Herklaas van Wyk replied, "that I must have lain asleep on the floor of that rondavel all those years. That must have been just at the end of the Boer War. And it's funny that I didn't wake up before my nation again needed me."

The rebels received the old man's last remark in silence. They were beginning to doubt the wisdom of their armed rising. They had been driven from pillar to post for many days. Incessant rain had damped their ardour.

"Did you remember to wind your watch before you went to sleep in that rondavel, Oom Herklaas?" Jan Gouws asked, trying to change the subject.

The others did not laugh at this sally. For one thing, the rain had started coming down again. . .

Some of the rebels seemed half-inclined to believe Herklaas van Wyk's story. And there seemed to be something inexplicably solemn in the thought of a burgher of the Transvaal Republic going to sleep in the corner of a deserted rondavel, with his Mauser at his side – and only waking up again a dozen years later, when men were once more riding with rifles slung across their shoulders.

"Did you dream at all during that time, Oom Herklaas?" another man asked, in a half-serious tone.

The old man thought for a little while.

"I remember dreaming about a mossie settling on a kaffir-boom that was full of red flowers," Herklaas van Wyk answered slowly, "but I think I dreamt of it a long time back – after I had been asleep only four years, or so."

Jan Gouws shivered. The red flowers on that kaffir-boom must be pretty well faded by now, he thought. And it gave him a queer feeling to think of that mossie, that an old man saw in a dream, flitting about in the sunshine of long ago. It made Jan Gouws feel uncomfortable, for a reason that he could not explain.

"My Mauser is very rusty," Herklaas van Wyk continued. "I've tried oiling it, but that doesn't help. I'll have to hands-up or shoot one of the enemy, and take his Lee-Metford off him, like we used to do. How long will it take us to win this war, do you think?"

The rebels did not answer. They knew that their cause was already shot to pieces. In spite of the old man's senility, there seemed to emanate from his spirit a strange kind of assurance, a form of steadfastness in the face of adversity and defeat that they themselves did not possess. It seemed that there was something inside the entrails of this burgher of the Transvaal Republic that they didn't have. Something firm and constant that they had lost. And they felt, sensing the difference between the previous generation and their own, and without being able to express their feelings in words, that in that difference lay their defeat.

"What happened about your horse, Oom Herklaas?" a young rebel asked eventually.

Outwardly dilapidated, Herklaas van Wyk still seemed to represent, somehow, the gloom and grandeur of a greater day.

"I had tethered my horse to a thorn-tree," Herklaas van Wyk said, "and he, too, must have fallen asleep. And I am sure that the hoof-beats of a commando at full gallop must have awakened him, also. For when I got to the thorn-tree – which hadn't grown much during that time: you know how slowly a thorn-tree grows – my old war-horse was sniffing the wind and pawing the ground. And his neck was arched."

The Heart of a Woman

BEFORE the kaffirs had guessed the significance of the aasvoëls wheeling about the Rooiwolk krans, Lettie Prinsloo had known, through a swift intuition, that the body of her husband, Gerhardus, would be lying in the thick bush at the foot of the krans. Gerhardus Prinsloo had been away from home for two days. He had walked out of the house without a word to his wife, Lettie. He hadn't said that he was going out to look for stray cattle.

Latterly Gerhardus had not spoken much to Lettie. Above all, he had not spoken of his elder brother, Arndt, who had returned to the Marico a few months ago, after having been in Johannesburg for several years, and was now living as a bywoner on Flip Bekker's farm, a couple of miles away.

When she saw those aasvoëls, black against the sky, wheeling in slow curves above the bush, Lettie Prinsloo knew immediately that the body of her husband Gerhardus would be lying at the foot of the krans. She hurried out of the house. She climbed through the barbed-wire fence of the cattle-kraal and when she came to the wall of the dam she started running.

And from then onwards Lettie Prinsloo ran all the way, tearing her blue cotton frock on the wag-'n-bietjie thorns and getting her legs scratched on the bushes – making her way through the yellow grass and over the uneven ground to the spot in the thick clump of bush at the foot of Rooiwolk krans, where lay the broken body of her husband, Gerhardus Prinsloo.

A couple of kaffirs working on the Prinsloos' farm saw the missus hurrying over the veld. So they followed after her, but at a respectful distance. The disappearance of Gerhardus Prinsloo from the farmstead a few days before had enabled the kaffirs to relax from their work on the lands, and so they were sitting by the side of a hut when Lettie Prinsloo came past. They were seated on their haunches against the wall of the hut, and they moved only as the sun moved. They knew how to make the best use of the temporary leisure afforded them by the absence of the baas, for they belonged to the Makhatla tribe, whose members are addicted to dagga-smoking in large quantities.

Now, seeing the missus running through the thorns like that, in the heat of the day, the two Bakhatlas put their pipe aside, for another occasion, and followed after Lettie Prinsloo at a respectful distance.

In the telling of this story I am puzzled by one or two things. What is it, for instance, that makes a woman favour one of her sons above the other? And why is it that the things that happen out of a situation like this are always more or less the same? Because this story of the two brothers, Arndt and Gerhardus Prinsloo, is no other than the story (with the characters in this order) of Esau and Jacob. And so I don't want to waste any unnecessary time on providing a resumé of a set of events so perfectly chronicled in Genesis XXV–XXVII.

I only wish to comment on certain features of the history of Arndt and Gerhardus Prinsloo, which is also the history of Esau and Jacob Ben-Isaac. And I would say that no man knows what it is in the heart of a woman, that thing chronicled in Genesis – "but Rebekah loved Jacob" – how that thing is tangled with the darkness of the womb and how it has roots in the primordial passions that surge out of the black earth and the red earth.

The Night-dress

JOHANNA Snyman stood in front of the kitchen table on which lay a pile of washing. It was ordinary farm clothing; her father's and brothers' blue jean shirts and trousers, her mother's and her own dresses and underwear.

Johanna took an iron off the stove, tilted it sideways and spat on it to see if it was hot. Then she went back to the table and commenced ironing.

It was a hot day in the Marico Bushveld. The heat from the sun and from the stove made the kitchen unbearable for Johanna's mother, who had gone to sit in front of the house with some sewing and a back number of the *Kerkbode*. Johanna's mother was known all over the district as Tant Lettie. She was thin and sallow-looking and complained regularly about her health. There was something the matter with her which rooi laventel, wit dulsies and other Boer remedies could not cure.

On the other hand, Johanna was strong and robustly made. Now, with the heat of the kitchen, there was a pink glow on her features. It was a flush that extended from her forehead right down to her neck and that part of her bosom which the blue print frock did not conceal. Her face was full and had just that tendency towards roundness that is much admired by the men of the Bushveld. But her nose was too small and too snub to remain attractive long after girlhood. And Johanna was twenty-three.

Tant Lettie, having put aside the *Kerkbode*, began embroidering a piece of cheap material that she had bought from the Indian store at Ramoutsa. She was making herself a night-dress. She held the partly finished garment to the light and examined it. She laughed softly. But it was not a meaningless laugh. There was too much bitterness in it for that. She wondered why she was taking all that trouble with her night-dress, sewing bits of pink tape on it and working French knots round the neck, for all the world as though she was making it for her honeymoon.

She remembered the time she got married. Twenty-four years ago. A long while beforehand she had made herself clothes. That was on the Highveld, in the Potchefstroom District. Her father had sold some oxen to the Jew trader and had given her the money to buy things for her marriage. That was a good time. She remembered that one night-dress she made. It was very fine stuff that cost a riksdaler a yard. She sewed on a lot of lace, and put in all kinds of tucks and frills. When it was finished it was pretty. She ironed it out and put it right at the bottom of the kist in her bedroom. She didn't want any of her brothers or sisters to see that night-dress, because they would make improper jokes about it and she would feel uncomfortable. As it was, they already had too much to say.

They went by Cape-cart to Potchefstroom for the wedding. Frans Snyman looked very happy. But he was excited and she was afraid he would drop the ring, and that would bring them bad luck. But he did not drop it, and yet they seemed to have got bad luck all the same. When the ceremony was over, Frans kissed her and said: "Now you will always be my wife." She felt afraid when he said that.

That night they stayed at her father's house. Then she and Frans left for the Government farm that Frans had bought in the Marico Bushveld. She remembered the way she had taken the night-dress out of the kist that evening after the wedding, and how she had laughed at the frills in it, and the ribbons and the lace, and had suddenly folded up the garment and pressed it against her breasts. But that was long ago.

She had kept the night-dress for many years. Often she looked at it and thought of the time when she had first worn it. But, somehow, it didn't seem the same. Each time she took it out it meant less to her than before. Afterwards she made a petticoat out of it for Johanna.

First Johanna was born. Then came, in turn, Willem and Adriaan and Lourens. In the first year of their marriage there was a big drought, and it was only after half the stock had died that Frans decided to trek with the remainder of the stock to the Limpopo River. It was in the ox-wagon that Johanna was born. Tant Lettie remembered that she was alone nearly all that day, with only a kaffir woman to attend to her. And Frans was in a bad temper because the kaffirs had been negligent and had allowed some oxen to get lost. Frans was also angry because she had not given birth to a man-child. He swore about it, as though it was her fault.

Later on, when Willem was born, Frans seemed a little more satisfied. But it was only for a while. There were other things that he had to concern himself with. It had rained and he had to sow mealies all day as long as the ground remained wet. As for the two youngest children, Adriaan and Lourens, Frans hardly noticed their coming.

Still, that was the way Frans was, and all men were like that. She knew he was sorry he had got married, and she didn't blame him for it. Only she thought that he need not always show it in such an open sort of way. For that matter, she was sorry also that she had got married. It would have been better if she had remained in her father's house. She knew she would have been unhappy there, and when her parents died she would have to go out and stay with somebody else. Or she might have been able to get work somewhere. But still, all that would have been much better than to get married. Now she had brought four children into the world who would lead the same kind of life that she had led.

Tant Lettie put down her sewing. Her face turned slightly pale. Her hands dropped to her sides. She felt, coming on once more, that pain which rooi laventel and wit dulsies could not cure.

In the kitchen Johanna had at last finished with the washing. Then she slipped quietly into her bedroom and came back with a garment which she unfolded in a way that had tenderness in it. She ran her fingers over the new linen, with the lace and ribbons and frills. Then, having ironed it, she took the night-dress to her bedroom and packed it away carefully at the bottom of her kist.

In Church

NSIDE the schoolroom at Droogtebult there was the smell of cheap
scent and stale powder mixed with sweat. The room was crowded on
that Sunday morning, for a church service between the quarterly
Nagmaals was an unusual event. There were present members of both
Dutch churches, the Hervormde and the Gereformeerde, and the min-
ster gave out only psalms, as he did not wish to antagonise the Dop-
pers, who do not sing hymns.

Gerhardina Brink sat at the end of a row of school benches. In that
same row were her father and mother and her younger brothers and sis-
ers. Gerhardina was the eldest of Thys Brink's children. She was six-
teen. But already there was a fullness about her breasts and a maturity
of development about her hips that elsewhere would be associated with
a woman much older than Gerhardina. The Bushveld sun, ripening the
kaffir-corn and the mealies, also ripened the women very early, perhaps even before their time. Already there had been young men who
had courted Thys Brink's daughter. There was the new school-teacher,
for instance, who had come often to the farm and had sat up with Gerhardina. But lately he had stayed away. It was rumoured that he had ap-
plied to the Education Department for a transfer to a school on the
Highveld. They said that the Bushveld climate did not agree with him.

While they were singing "Prys den Heer", Gerhardina looked up
from the book and encountered the gaze of the school-teacher. She had
tried often during the service to catch his eye, but always he had seemed to look past her. But now there was no doubt about it. She had looked at him at the same time that he had looked at her. Yes, he had seen
her, right enough. . . and all he did was to turn his head away quickly
and stare at something on the wall. Suddenly Gerhardina felt a sickness
within her. She heard her father's voice droning the words of the psalm
through his beard. She saw Lena van Heerden glance at her strangely
and she blushed. She watched the minister putting slips of paper in his
Bible for place-marks. And all the time within her was that terribly sick
feeling.

She was relieved when the singing was over and she could sit down
again.

The minister was a young man who had only recently qualified at
the Potchefstroom Theological Seminary. He was obviously nervous.

He cleared his throat frequently and stuttered even in reading the text. But the people to whom he preached had a respect for all ministers. It was a reverence that stretched back for many generations. It was older than the Transvaal Republic. It was older than the Great Trek. It was older than Van Riebeeck. So now though the minister stuttered and was nervous, the congregation did not notice it.

"Sing, O barren, thou that didst not bear," he read. "Break forth into singing and cry aloud, thou that didst not travail with child."

Gerhardina listened to these words. Somehow, she felt that she understood what those words meant, in a way that the minister could not understand them. She felt that it was just as though she had all at once become an old woman. The minister went on to talk about Isaiah, but she did not hear him. Again she glanced hurriedly at the schoolteacher, but he must have expected something like that, because his face was still turned away from her, and he was still studying that part of the wall. The minister kept talking, his nervousness beginning to wear off. Near the back a baby in arms started crying. It was a thin, pitiful sort of wail, and everybody turned round, as though they had never before heard a child cry. The mother rocked the baby to and fro in an effort to soothe it, but without success; she then walked out and stood in the sun in front of the door and nuzzled the child at her breast. A number of men near the door turned round and watched the operation idly.

"Thou that didst not travail with child," Gerhardina murmured to herself. She wondered if Lena van Heerden really had looked at her in a peculiar way, or if she had only imagined it. But there was no imagination about the way in which the teacher had purposely tried to avoid her.

Then she looked at her father and mother. She wondered how many times she had seen her father sit just that way in church, his shoulders hunched forward, his eyes half closed, his black coat – which with age was becoming green in places – sprinkled at the collar with dandruff. Her mother had a handkerchief up to her eyes. There never yet had been a sermon preached that did not move her mother.

Gerhardina was pleased when the last psalm had been sung and the minister had pronounced the blessing. She walked on alone to the mule-cart which was standing under a thorn-tree. Her parents remained around the school building for a while, talking to different people. Also, her father was anxious to get in a word with the minister, because if people saw him conversing with the minister in an intimate kind of way it would help his chances of getting nominated as ouderling. Her brothers and sisters stayed with their parents, but Gerhardina wanted to be alone.

"I saw that school-teacher," her father said when they had got into the cart. "He was talking to Frikkie Haasbroek. When I came along he slunk away like a dog that steals fat. He doesn't come to see you any more, either. If he thinks we're not good enough for him, he can. . . "

So her father went on.

Why couldn't people understand? Gerhardina wondered. Still, they would know one of these days. She couldn't go on concealing it much longer. Already, it seemed that Lena van Heerden looked at her as if she knew. Yet it didn't matter. There was always a way out.

But on the road back to the farm Gerhardina admitted to herself that, when the time came, she would lack the courage to drink sheep-dip, like Sophie Lombard had done when she was with child.

Politics and Love

ON the blackboard that you could see every time the speaker moved his head to one side was a multiplication sum: 973 x 8 = . There had been a number there, after the equals, but the schoolmaster had rubbed it out quickly, before the first members of the audience filed into the classroom for the meeting.

It was just possible that the answer wasn't quite correct, the schoolmaster reflected, and he didn't want any nonsense about it from some busybody, afterwards.

The schoolmaster did not feel called upon to erase, from the blackboard, a brief statement to do with the geographical regions traversed by the Vaal River.

Thus it came about that every time Lennep van Ploert, the representative for Bekkersdal, moved his head to one side or the other, or bent forward to think – which he did not appear to do very deeply – there was revealed behind him, on the blackboard, in addition to the arithmetic, this sentence whose truth few would question, or, rather (this being a political meeting) would cavil at: "The Vaal River is in Africa."

Lennep van Ploert wore a black suit and a high, stick-up collar. And his voice was just as impressive as his looks. Many of the farmers and their wives present at the meeting had received their education in that same classroom and sitting on those same benches. Consequently, more than one member of the audience identified Lennep van Ploert in his mind with the Hollander school inspector who had come round annually to tell the pupils whether they had passed or failed.

There was a good attendance of farmers and their wives and children from the Rooibokspruit area to hear Lennep van Ploert report, in that schoolroom that served for a night as a political party venue, on the way he had furthered his constituents' interests during the past year in a building of more imposing dimensions than the schoolhouse, and with statelier portals.

Another point of difference between the two buildings was that in the Marico schoolroom the older pupils seldom threw chalk, any more. Most of them had also learnt to reject the cruder formularies of comedy built up around the placing of drawing pins on the schoolmaster's chair.

"And so in your interests I went and had tea with the Marquis de

Monfiche," the voice of Lennep van Ploert boomed. "And while I was drinking tea with that distinguished French aristocrat and insurance representative – "

"Are you sure it was tea?" a man in a khaki shirt sitting at the back of the classroom interjected.

A couple of people in the audience giggled. Others said "Sh— " Among the latter was the wife of a wealthy local cattle-smuggler. She was hoping that Lennep van Ploert would go on to say how the wife of the distinguished French marquis was dressed.

The only person who was in no way embarrassed was the speaker himself. The remark made by the man in the khaki shirt was of a pattern accepted as wit in that other building (the one with the proud traditions and the coat of arms over the front stoep). Lennep van Ploert felt at home, then.

"No, it wasn't tea," the speaker said. "It was a milkshake."

In that noble edifice in which Lennep van Ploert shone as a debater, such a brilliant piece of repartee would have received due appreciation. Grim features would have relaxed in smiles. A policeman wearing white gloves would have gone to the assistance of an elderly legislator who was in stitches through laughing.

There would have been jovial shouts of "Withdraw!" There would have been a row of stipples in Hansard, the short-hand reporter not being able to get down the next couple of sentences on account of his emotions being so mixed. And afterwards, in the lobby, even some of Lennep van Ploert's opponents would have come and grasped Lennep van Ploert by the hand.

But, singularly enough, in that Marico schoolroom with the whitewashed walls and the thatched roof and with no inspiring statuary on the premises – unless a child's clay model on a window-sill of Adam with a pipe and braces could fit into that category (one of Adam's braces having slipped off his shoulder on to a level with his knee) – in that Marico classroom there was no immediate response of the sort that Lennep van Ploert had looked for.

Instead, the audience started wondering if there was something that they had missed, perhaps, in what Lennep van Ploert had just said. Or was he taking them to be just a lot of simpletons, because they were living out in the most northern part of the Bushveld that you could live in and still be allowed to vote?

The only positive reaction, however, came from the man in the khaki shirt. He vacated his place at the back of the schoolroom and moved up to a seat nearer the front.

"After I had signed the insurance papers for an endowment policy," Lennep van Ploert proceeded, "the French marquis said he would be honoured if my wife and I would visit him at his chateau next time we were in France. He did not know exactly when he would be going back to France, though. The marquis told me straight out that there was something about South Africa that he *liked*. Anyway, I told him that, speaking on behalf of my constituents, I would accept his invitation." (Applause.)

The man in the khaki shirt had been sitting between a young fellow with a blue and orange tie and a young girl with a selon's rose in her hair.

The young man looked sideways at the girl and even in the uncertain light of the paraffin lamps the flush on his face was evident. The redness extended to the top part of his ears.

"I can't hear too well from there," the young fellow explained, moving into the seat vacated by the man with the khaki shirt.

The girl did not answer.

"Is he – is he your father?" the young man enquired in a faltering voice, at the same time indicating the man in the khaki shirt, who was then engaged in feeling through his trousers pockets, thereby occasioning noticeable discomfort to the farmer sitting next to him, by reason of the confinement imposed by the school bench.

"He's my uncle," the girl answered. "I stay with him. I lost my parents when I was young."

"I have before today tried to speak to you," the young fellow with the blue and orange tie went on. "But he was always with you."

"I know," the girl answered, unconsciously putting her hand up to the selon's rose in her hair.

"At Zeerust with the last Nagmaal, now," the young man went on. "By the side of the kerkplein."

"Yes," the girl responded, simply.

"Only, your uncle kicked out, then, at – " the young man proceeded.

"He kicked just at a wild berry," the girl explained. "He's been like that since he came back from the mines."

"Well, I just didn't understand, then," the young man said. "My name is Dawie Louw. What's yours?"

"Lettie," the girl answered.

"Well, it was because your uncle kicked out, like that," Dawie Louw went on, "that I didn't – "

"Didn't come up and speak to us," Lettie helped him out.

"Yes, and I think Lettie is a lovely name," the young fellow said.

"And I like the name Dawie, also," the girl said in a soft voice.

"And there was another time when I nearly came up and spoke to you," Dawie Louw went on. "It was right in front of – "

"Solly's hardware store," Lettie said. "Next to the four-disc harrows."

From her voice it sounded like it was the rose garden of the Capulets under a Veronese moon.

"That's right," Dawie Louw said. "Only your uncle was again with you, and just when I was coming up, after pulling my tie straight – it was a purple tie with – "

"Green spots," Lettie announced, looking slightly pained.

"Well," Dawie Louw said, "just as I was coming up, your uncle – "

"Kicked out at a four-disc harrow's disc," Lettie said. "That's another habit my uncle has brought back from the mines. He also carries a bicycle chain, through having lived in Fordsburg."

Meanwhile, on the platform, Lennep van Ploert was continuing with his report to his constituents of his legislative activities.

" – wlawlawski," Lennep van Ploert was saying. "And it was coffee I had with him, that time, I mean with that distinguished Polish prince, who happened to have a few shares in a washing machine company to dispose of, at the moment, and that I purchased. He invited me, on behalf of my constituents, to drop in at his palace in Poland whenever I was passing that way. But he didn't think he would go back there himself quite soon, the prince said. For one thing, he *liked* South Africa, he said. And he also mentioned something about their just *waiting* for him to come back, in his native country of Poland."

The man in the khaki shirt, Lettie's uncle, spoke up for himself, then.

"Could they give my trousers a bit of a press?" he asked. "That Polish washing machine company of yours, that is?"

At the same time the man in the khaki shirt got up and moved to a seat that was still nearer the front.

"Has your uncle had – " Dawie Louw asked of Lettie.

"A few too many? Yes, I think so. It's since," Lettie said, once more, "he's come back from the mines."

Dawie Louw asked the girl with the selon's rose in her hair if she didn't think it was a queer thing that, after all that, they should at last have the chance of meeting and of talking to each other, sitting right next to each other on a school bench, even.

He was young and sanguine, then, and he didn't know that a school bench actually was the right place where two young lovers should meet. For who would yet have more to learn of the ways of the world than a boy and girl in love?

"Praat politiek," somebody shouted out to Lennep van Ploert. It was not the man in the khaki shirt (Lettie's uncle) that shouted. It was some other farmer, who had come to hear about policy and about election promises, and who couldn't understand that Lennep van Ploert, who had been such a firebrand a few years before, should now be content to hand out milksop stuff. For Lennep van Ploert was now talking about when he had cocoa with a Spanish nobleman who did a spot of real estate agency work in his spare time.

Lennep van Ploert leant forward to think, for a few moments, then.

And so Dawie Louw and Lettie were able to see what was written on the blackboard. And they spelt out, between them, the statement that the Vaal River was in Africa. And they laughed – just for no reason at all. They did not know that they would have been far better occupied in working out that arithmetic sum, instead. But young people in love don't know that at the time, of course. They think they know better.

"The first time I saw you was at the fat stock sale at Schooneesdrif," Dawie Louw said to Lettie. "You were with your uncle and you wouldn't look at me."

"The first time I saw you," Lettie said, "was before Schooneesdrif."

"At Schooneesdrif you had on a frock with – " Dawie Louw started again.

But it was as much at Lettie's suggestion as his own that they slipped out of the door of the classroom, then, the two of them together, hand in hand. And they stood like that, a long time, hand in hand, in silence, under the unclothed stars.

That was how they came to miss the unhappy incidents that took place inside the schoolroom a little later. For the man in the khaki shirt (Lettie's uncle) had eventually found what he was looking for, in his trousers pocket. But he was pulled off Lennep van Ploert before he could assault him to any serious purpose with his bicycle chain. But before that Lettie's uncle had borne the legislator back against the blackboard.

And that was how the meeting ended. And, strangely enough, although Lennep van Ploert represented, for many members of the audience, the school inspector of their youth, they were not unwilling to forgive the man in the khaki shirt for having dealt with him in that fashion.

Because of the way he had been pressed backwards against the blackboard by Lettie's uncle, you were able to read afterwards, on Lennep van Ploert's suit – the figures being the wrong way around – part of the sum in arithmetic. What was also legible on Lennep van Ploert's jacket – reading from right to left – was a chalked statement to the effect that the Vaal River flows in Africa.

But of neither of these circumstances did Dawie Louw and Lettie know anything. They stood at the side of the schoolhouse, holding hands under the stars. And they were young. And they were in love. And they were foolish. And they would not have cared about what vital sort of decision any statesman would have arrived at, then.

And they would have laughed about any Parallel that any general might have decided to cross.

New Elder

"THIS is Elder Haasbroek," Wynand Geel said, and we shook hands all round.

"He is the new elder from – " Wynand Geel began again, when Hans Combrinck broke into a laugh. The rest of us laughed, also. It sounded funny, *"new elder."* The only one that didn't laugh was the new elder himself. He drew himself up straight and you could see from his manner that he thought people from our part of the Groot Marico were somewhat easily amused. Childishly easy, sort of.

Wynand Geel started trying to explain to Elder Haasbroek.

"Why they are laughing," he said, "is because it sounded, well, something to laugh at, you know – saying, *'nuwe ouderling'.*"

"Yes," Elder Haasbroek answered, "oh, yes, I see. Quite."

Even without Wynand Geel having introduced him, however, we would have known that he was an elder. And we would still have known it if he had had on ordinary farm clothes, instead of the black manel suit with the white tie that he was wearing.

We got in each other's way, finding seats on Wynand Geel's stoep. For Elder Haasbroek had taken the armchair that Oom Doors Perskes usually occupied, and so we had all of us to shift into different places, and we sat upright.

We heard Wynand Geel's daughter moving about in the front bedroom. Wynand called her.

"I suppose you'll have the usual little old Bushveld refreshment, Elder?" Wynand Geel asked Elder Haasbroek.

When Drieka came out on to the stoep we understood what she had been doing in the bedroom. Her hair was now fastened back with a pink ribbon. Before Wynand Geel could ask her if she had coffee on the stove, Elder Haasbroek spoke.

"Well, I was thinking that it was perhaps a bit early in the morning," Elder Haasbroek said to Wynand Geel. "But I have heard that it is a custom you have here in this part of the Groot Marico. So I won't offend you. Make mine just three inches of peach mampoer."

"Mamp–" Hans Combrinck started to blurt out in surprise, stopping himself halfway, however.

By that time it was too late for Wynand Geel to explain that he had meant coffee, and that we weren't used to taking anything stronger at that time of the day. Wynand went into the voorhuis himself and fetched out glasses and a bottle. There have probably never been any more astonished Groot Marico farmers than that little group that sat on the front stoep, in the forenoon, drinking mampoer, with an elder of the church in their midst.

A little later, Wynand Geel fetched out another bottle.

After Elder Haasbroek had gone, we said that when Wynand Geel had spoken of him as a new elder, he hadn't been so far wrong. He was at all events a new *sort* of elder.

We learnt that, some time later, Elder Haasbroek again called at Wynand Geel's home, with a couple of tracts. And Wynand was away in Zeerust, as Drieka told him when she answered the door. And Elder Haasbroek stayed quite a long time.

We realised, then, that Elder Haasbroek was not such a new sort of elder, after all.

Shy Young Man

HANS Combrinck nudged Chris van Blerk.

"Why don't you ask Wynand now – like you said you would?" Hans wanted to know.

Because he was young, and diffident, Chris van Blerk mumbled something about there being so many people sitting here on the stoep smoking their pipes and drinking coffee and about it perhaps being better if he spoke to Oom Wynand Geel about it afterwards, when there weren't so many people sitting here on the stoep drinking their pipes and smoking – at least, what he meant to say was – His mumble got lost in the sound of coffee being poured into saucers and the rattle of crockery.

Hans Combrinck laughed.

"What do you think of that, Wynand?" he asked. "I told Chris van Blerk last week that he would come right as far as your house, and he would sit here on your stoep, with his one veldskoen on the support of a chair, just like he's doing now, and he still wouldn't ask you."

Immediately Oom Doors Perskes started talking about the old days, when you were fully grown up, with adult responsibilities, by the age of fifteen, and you could distil your own moepel brandy by the time you were twelve. So there wasn't such a thing as a shy young man in the old days, Oom Doors said. Indeed, there wasn't such a thing as a young man at all. Not when you had to cure your own chewing tobacco before you were ten and grind up your own snuff before you were two, Oom Doors said. He forgot now at what a ridiculously early age you would have to shoot your own Mshangaan.

"What I can remember, though, is the time they needed an assistant magistrate for the Pilanesberg," Oom Doors Perskes went on. "The old landdrost couldn't cope with all the work himself anymore, as he was getting on in years. He was close on to thirty, I think. Well, somebody had to step in, and we felt it was up to the Perskes family. My father was too old, of course. In fact, he was, if anything, even older than the old landdrost. Moreover, my father couldn't spell long words. Still, in that respect he wasn't much different from the old landdrost, who, I believe, couldn't spell at all. My elder brothers were busy deepening the Molopo River and throwing a barrage across it. So I had to go."

"I suppose you were about eleven, then, when you became a magistrate?" Hans Combrinck asked, sarcastically.

"Eleven and a half," Oom Doors Perskes replied. "My younger brother couldn't take on the job because the part he was playing in politics at that time made him an unsuitable candidate for the judiciary. But, anyway, that's how we were in those days. Men. No want of confidence. Sure of ourselves."

Drieka Geel came on to the stoep with the tray to collect the cups and saucers.

"You've been doing it *again*," she said when she came to where Oom Doors Perskes was sitting. "Knocking out your pipe on the arm of this chair that I've got to polish with olieblaar."

Oom Doors looked abject. Then he stammered out some lie by way of excuse, saying that it was maybe somebody else that had knocked out his pipe on the arm of the chair.

When we were leaving, Wynand Geel took Chris van Blerk slightly aside and replied to the question that Chris had not put to him. "Better ask her yourself," Wynand Geel said.

Night on the Veld

"IT's a boundless universe," Frikkie Terblans, the school-teacher said, looking up at the stars through the leaves of a kameeldoring.

Gysbert van Tonder was suitably impressed. He pulled the blankets closer about his neck. Whatever the schoolmaster might say, now, Gysbert van Tonder, with sleep beginning to steal over him, was determined to make his own universe as cosy and as limited as possible.

"Talking about stars," Jan Wessels said, "well, I remember Halley's comet, all right. My mother held me up to the window to have a look at it. She said that she would never live to see it again, but that I might – with luck. I don't know where she got her information from. They didn't have wireless sets in those days. And I don't think they would have said anything about Halley's comet in the *Dagblad* of that time. I mean, it was so soon after the Boer War. The last thing the *Dagblad* would have written about would have been an English comet. All the same, my mother said that she would be dead before Halley's comet came round again. It would take such a long time, she explained. I forget how many years. But it's a funny thing that when I went to round up my donkeys, one night, by the Molopo, and I fell over a lion while I was carrying a lantern, and all – you know, in the dark I mistook that lion for a donkey: it wasn't a very good lantern – anyway, then, all of a sudden, what my mother told me as a child came back to me. And I could *see* Halley's comet, while I was running. That lion was asleep, fortunately."

Jurie Bekker cleared his throat. We could sense what Jurie Bekker wanted to say. But we could also appreciate Jurie Bekker's difficulty. Jurie Bekker naturally wanted to call the accuracy of Jan Wessels's story in question. But he didn't quite know how to do it, without seeming perhaps to insult the memory of Jan Wessels's late mother.

We understood then, again, something of the cunning of Jan Wessels's mind. For Jan Wessels was known from the Bechuanaland border to as far as Vleisfontein for the low quickness of his brain, which we admired very much, and which we said should get him into the Volksraad, some day, where he would be at least a minister.

In having brought his mother into his lion story in that way, right at the start, Jan Wessels made it difficult for us to say, straight out, what we really thought of his story.

Jurie Bekker solved the problem after this fashion.

"Well, it's nice, Jan," Jurie Bekker said, clearing his throat again, "it's nice to think that you survived that. I mean, you've got a good chance of seeing that comet again, some day. Some night, rather, I should say."

Jan Wessels reflected for a few moments.

"Of course," he acknowledged, judiciously, "of course, the reason that the lion didn't do much about it, then, was because he happened to be asleep."

Frikkie Terblans, the school-teacher, who was always strong on facts, would not allow a statement like that to pass unchallenged.

"Who has ever heard," Frik Terblans demanded, "of a lion being asleep at night?"

"Well, maybe it was a sick lion," Jan Wessels hastened to explain. "Maybe the lion was sick and had gone to lie down for a bit, to try and get better. You know what lions are. He must have had lion sickness."

"Lion sickness," Gysbert van Tonder repeated, sleepily, starting to snore the moment afterwards. It was a pretty healthy kind of snore.

"Better help Gysbert turn over," Jurie Bekker said. "It sounds like a lion that's just made a kill, the way he's snoring. We don't want the hyenas to come around us. From the noises Gysbert is making, the hyenas will think that there will be some pieces of left-over ribbok here, shortly. You know how ignorant a hyena is."

Jurie Bekker got up, then. And because he had not taken off his veldskoens before going to bed, he was able quite easily to help Gysbert van Tonder to turn round. In fact, Gysbert van Tonder turned round almost twice, the way Jurie Bekker helped him.

By that time Frikkie Terblans, the school-teacher from Drogevlei, who had come on this hunting expedition with us, was again looking up at the stars.

Now, you can say what you like about other countries' stars, but there's one thing about the stars that you see in the sky over South Africa. The right way to see them is through the narrow, dim leaves of a kameeldoring. They look like stars, then, when you are lying on your back, and quite near at hand there is a camp-fire consisting of the burning part of one end of a withaak trunk that the white ants have been eating for the last eighteen years or so. When once you've got that withaak tree-trunk burning you're all right. All you need do after that is, at intervals, to move the tree-trunk forward some more into the flames part with your foot.

That was what Jurie Bekker did then before going back to lie down in his blankets. He assisted that tree-trunk to burn better in the same manner that he had aided Gysbert van Tonder to stop snoring.

All in all, it was a pretty active night for Jurie Bekker.

A large number of yellow sparks shot skywards, then.

The sparks rose upwards among the thorns and leaves. Afterwards they blended, the sparks in the moment of their dying, with the other sparks of burning flame that was the Milky Way – *they* being destined to light the paths of men a little longer, the sparks of the sidereal skies.

"The stars," Frikkie Terblans, the school-teacher, said, after a while, bringing us back to where we had started from. And he spoke about the spectrum and about how it broke up into seven colours the light of any star that ever was. The spectrum explained away just every star that shone in the skies, Frik Terblans said. It was a simple matter of a glass prism. From that you could tell how much magnesium and hydrogen and sodium and calcium there was in a star, even though you saw that star through summer leaves and thin thorns.

Jurie Bekker got up again and kicked the withaak some more. While he was about it he also induced Gysbert van Tonder – who had started snoring again – to turn over. Gysbert van Tonder turned over twice, in fact, and somewhat quickly. We felt that Jurie Bekker acted a bit short-tempered, that time.

Although Gysbert van Tonder had been silenced, that part of the night in which we were lying was not really still. There were rustling sounds in the grass. Mostly, that was insects. Occasionally, one or two of them would get in underneath your blankets. I felt I would like the schoolmaster to look through the spectroscope and tell me how much potassium and mixed gases there was in those insects – provided only that he would catch them first. Because that was the hard part.

There was a stirring in the trees. It was the night wind, only. And then there came, floating on the bosom of the night wind, a series of weird bushveld noises. It was not the sort of noise that would upset one, of course. But there was a strange sort of element in it. What made the noise unusual, kind of, was that part of it was a *hushed* noise. The other part of it was not so hushed.

"Queer how much a leopard likes monkey," Jan Wessels observed, in a quite nonchalant fashion. "That's something I can't understand, now. Have you ever tasted monkey? No? Well, I *have*. And I think nothing at all of monkey taste. What's more, I don't care who knows it, either.

Mind you, I don't say that grilled baboon chop isn't all right. Nothing marvellous, mind you. Nevertheless, you can *eat* it. That's where monkey is different. So I just can't understand the way a leopard carries on when he's got a bit of monkey. Just listen to that, now. No, not *that*. That's just the monkey. Ah, did you hear that? That deep growl – satisfied-sounding, sort of. No, *not* that. That's the monkey, as I told you, man. Hark, there it is again. Iggou–gou–ggg – did you catch it? Your ear has to become pretty finely attuned to bushveld sounds to enable you to hear iggou–gou–ggg from a distance. No, *not* that other sound – I've already told you: that's the *monkey*. He's making those other sounds. He won't be making them much longer, I should imagine. I mean, judging by all those iggou–gou–ggg sounds, I mean. But what on earth a leopard can *see* in a monkey beats me. . . Ah, well, you can hear hardly any monkey sound at *all*, now. . . "

"The stars," Frikkie Terblans, the school-teacher was saying again. . .

Old Transvaal Story

As Scully, I think, knew – have you ever chanced upon his "Ukushwama"? – the Transvaal seems to have had only one ghost story. It is a story that I have heard very often, told over and over again in voorkamer and by camp-fire, with the essential features always the same, and with only the details, in respect of characters and locale, differing with the mood and the personality – and the memory, perhaps – of each person that tells it.

The story of the Transvaal's only ghost goes something like this.

A solitary traveller on horseback enquires his way at a farmhouse after dark.

"That means you'll be going through the poort" (or the kloof or the drift, as the case may be) "at full moon," the farmer says to the traveller. "Well, no man has ever been able to ride his horse through that poort at night when the moon is full."

Actually, there is no need to tell the story any further than that. In those few words the farmer has said everything. . . A certain place along the road is haunted, and even if the traveller should not happen to notice the ghost – because he is thinking of something else, likely – the horse certainly *will* see the ghost, and will rear up on his hind legs. After that, neither whip nor spur, nor calling him by his first name, coaxingly, will get the horse past that spot where the spectre lurks.

Accordingly, the traveller turns back along the road he has come, riding quite fast, this time. And he arrives once more at that farmhouse where he received the unearthly warning in the first instance. The wise old farmer has known all along that the traveller would be back, of course, and after having persuaded him, without much difficulty, to spend the night there, proceeds to acquaint him in leisurely fashion over a jar of peach brandy with the circumstances that led to the poort becoming haunted.

This is a good story. I have heard it told – nearly always in the first person – by dozens of different people, always with only slight variations, and these of a strictly local character.

Indeed, I have heard this story so often, in different parts of the Transvaal, that it doesn't make my hair stand on end, any more. If the truth must be known, I've got somewhat blasé about the Transvaal's only ghost.

The result is that, nowadays, when a man says – lowering his voice and trying to make his tones sound sepulchral – "And so Oom Hannes Blignaut said to me that I would not be able to ride my horse through that poort in the full moon," I short-circuit him by asking, "But why didn't you go on a push-bike, instead?"

I have not, to date, found an answer to that one.

Similarly, as far as I have been able to discover, the Transvaal has got only one murder story – this, likewise, an amazingly good one. Only, through constant repetition, the gloss has for me been worn off this stirring old tale as well. I first heard it as a child; since then it has been related to me many times, as I am sure it has been to every South African who has spent some portion of his life on the Transvaal platteland. I suppose the story is based on historical fact: its salient features seem to relate to some murder that actually was committed long ago.

This story, I should like to add in parenthesis, has never been told to me in the first person. No man has ever said to me, "And so after I hit my wife with the chopper I buried her under the mud floor of the voorkamer and later on the police came."

For that, in rough outline, is the Transvaal's only murder story. It sounds bald, somehow, conveyed in those words. Put that way, it sounds more like a murder than like a murder story. But this old tale has a twist to it arising out of what happened in a certain period of time between the committing of the murder and the arrival of the police. The man has murdered his wife. . . Good. . . He has buried her under the floor of the voorkamer. . . Right. . . He proceeds to smooth over the broken portion of the floor with clay and moist cow-dung. . . Yes, excellent. All that seems straightforward enough.

But it is at this very point that the totally unexpected happens. This is the sensational development in the plot that distinguishes the Transvaal's only murder story from almost any other murder story I have ever lighted upon. For it is not two plain-clothes policemen that come walking into the voorkamer, in the early evening, when the murderer is down on his hands and knees putting the final touches to the restoration of the damaged floor. The time for the landdrost's men to arrive is not yet. But a couple of men do enter: only, they carry in bottles. They are followed by a number of girls who carry in the fragrance of romance with red veld-flowers in their hair. Then more men come in with bottles. And then a man with a concertina. And there is much laughter.

And more girls. Girls with names like Drieka and Tossie and Francina. It is a surprise party.

Of all things. . . Yes, of all the nights in the year, this man's neighbours had to choose just that particular night for throwing a surprise party in his house.

As I have said, this is the Transvaal's oldest – and, as far as I know, only – murder story. I heard it first as a child. Since then I have heard it many times. So have you, too, I suppose.

Like the one about the ghost in the poort, this is also a very good tale, and where it is particularly admirable, from the narrator's point of view, is that it lends itself to the introduction of an infinite variety of graceful and delicate touches in the psychological unfolding of the later scenes. Here great play can be made of the murderer's character. If he is somebody without much refinement and just says straight out, "I've buried my wife under the floor, there. This is no time for foolishness like dancing" – then the story has got to end right there, of course.

If he says, on the other hand, "I'm sorry, my wife went unexpectedly to Potchefstroom," and then allows the party to go on, trying to be as natural as possible, so as not to awaken unnecessary suspicions, then the subsequent developments offer charming possibilities.

To take, just at random, a single courthouse scene.

"And so you danced," the prosecutor would say to Kittie de Bruyn, one of the girls who was at that party. "Did it not come as a shock to you afterwards to think that you danced all night on the head of a dead woman?"

"But I danced lightly," Kittie de Bruyn would answer, "oh – lightly."

It is a situation providing lots of blossomy openings for fragile irony and high drama.

Incidentally, I, too, have told that story before of the woman interred under the floor of the voorkamer. And I have always known that I would have to dig her up again, some time. She was too useful a character to be left lying there, buried under four lines of prose.

The lack of imagination – or, perhaps, meagreness of event – that has bestowed upon the Transvaal only one ghost story and one murder story, does not apply in respect of love stories. The Transvaal has got hundreds of love stories, all opulently different. Woven on the common pattern of boy-meets-girl, one love story, in respect of its external shape, seems very much the same as another. And it is always at the very moment when you fancy that you have recognised the type of love story, when you have pigeon-holed it in your mind as belonging to such-and-such a category – it is at that very moment that you are betrayed; for, lo, there is sudden witchery, and a wand is waved, and it is as though a line of black dancers comes running in suddenly, and you find that a whole lot of people are laughing at you from behind the feathers and painted wood of their Congo masks.

One must be careful about classifying a love story, tabulating and cataloguing it as belonging to a certain sub-section of a particular group – indexing it and labelling it as conforming, in respect of characters and plot and incident, to a well-known and clearly recognised pattern.

Take the love story of Gideon Welman and Alie du Plessis, for instance. Superficially, it seems to conform to a pretty clearly defined type. A rustic idyll. The course of true love not running entirely smoothly. A vague suggestion of complications arising from the oldest geometrical symbol used in romance – the triangle, which is also the shape of the human heart. On the face of it, this is a simple kind of tale that you would be able to classify very easily. And yet, until almost the very end, Gideon Welman himself did not know what the pattern was into which his own love story fitted.

Gideon Welman and Alie du Plessis were seated under an ox-wagon. It was evening. A number of Boer families were trekking back to the Bushveld from the Nagmaal at Zeerust. Next time Gideon Welman and Alie du Plessis would be on that road they would be travelling down to Zeerust to get married. In a few months' time they would be spending their honeymoon on that same road, inside the ox-wagon under which they were at that moment seated. Alie du Plessis was now half-reclining against Gideon Welman, whose arms were about her. Her fingers were plucking at a tuft of smooth, strong grass. The light of the camp-fire flickered on their young faces. They were oblivious of the people around the fire, who were roasting mealies and telling stories. They were not, however, oblivious of the Bushveld night.

And it had to happen at that moment, while they were seated under the wagon, that Alie said something about Rooi Jan Venter.

"There you go again," Gideon Welman exclaimed. "Why have you got to keep on mentioning his name, anyway?"

The point is that Alie du Plessis cared for Gideon Welman, her bridegroom to be, deeply enough. It was not her fault that her feelings for him were not on a plane of ecstasy – were not in the nature of a romantic passion. She did not get a wild thrill at the name "Welman" – no relation of Gideon's – on the signboard of a butcher-shop in Zeerust. She did not flush tremulously when she saw, outspanned on the kerk-plein, a mule-cart whose infirm wheels proclaimed it to be Gideon's.

Not that Alie du Plessis did not have a very genuine affection for Gideon Welman, of course. But there you were. . .

Gideon's face was very white and tense in the flickering gleams of the camp-fire.

So Gideon Welman and Alie du Plessis were married in Zeerust. For a while – as far as the outside world was concerned, at least – they lived together happily in their little house in the Bushveld, with the newly whitewashed walls and the roof thatched with what was still last year's grass. And then events slid into that afternoon on which Gideon Welman was working very fast, and in a half-daze. He had the queer feeling that he was living in another life, going through a thing that had happened before, to somebody else, long ago. It was quite dark by the time a knock came at the door.

And when he got up from the floor quickly, dusting his knees, Gideon Welman knew what that old Transvaal story was, into whose pattern his own story had now fitted, also. For the door of the voorkamer opened. And out of the night came the laughter of girls. And Rooi Jan Venter and another young man entered the voorkamer, carrying bottles.

The Murderess

"ONE of your best friends, wasn't he, Frans?" Japie Krige asked of me in the Gouspoort post office after I had read the letter. "You knew them both well, didn't you?"

I nodded, recalling a time when there had been a similar letter in the post, but on *that* occasion not addressed to me. I now read the letter from Willem Lemmer's widow again:

> Dear Frans,
> You will no doubt be much grieved to learn that my husband is no more. During his last days he spoke of you often. Though he fought hard for life, he seemed to know the end was coming. Some time before his death Willem said to me: "Stoffelina, I would wish Frans to come here after I am gone that he may take for himself what he would like to have as a remembrance of me."
>
> I therefore write you of Willem's last wish that concerns you, and say that I would be glad if you could come to the farm when you are able.
>
> Stoffelina Lemmer
>
> P. S. The funeral was on Friday. Elder Duvenhage read from the Gospel of Mark and we sang from Psalm 18 three verses and from Hymn 27 the first and last verses. The elder spoke very beautifully of Willem.

I could not but recall the time when I had seen a very similar letter, but held in another's hands.

"Not so very old, either, was he?" Japie Krige remarked when we left the post office together.

I said, no, but it was an unhealthy area, that low-lying stretch in the fold of the 'Nwati hills.

"If you ask me," Japie Krige replied, "the whole of the Bushveld seems pretty unhealthy. If it's not malaria, it's leopards, or it's – "

Japie Krige was from the city. He and I were partners in a corundum proposition outside Gouspoort. And in spite of the way he talked, sometimes, decrying the necessarily primitive conditions of our mode of existence, the fact remained that he had adapted himself remarkably well to a life which, if it was rough, nevertheless offered a physical freedom that a city-dweller could know nothing of – and bestowed on the spirit a quality not of breadth but of intensity. To the mind of one living in the bush, the bush did strange things. One's imaginative faculties could not but be stimulated.

" – or it's snakes," Japie Krige went on. "Well, that's unhealthy enough, if you ask *me*."

Yet, in the main, with Japie Krige that sort of thing was just talk. And I suspected that, if he were ever presented with the opportunity of again establishing himself in the city, he would not take advantage of it. I felt that, in spite of what he said, the Bushveld had got into Japie Krige's blood, and that he would not quit it readily.

We walked down the dusty road of the Bechuana village of Gouspoort – of which the post office next to the native store was the most important building – on the way back to our camp. It was early afternoon. The heat was oppressive. Vast numbers of goats were sprawled about the place; lying in the half-shade of thorn-scrubs, pressing up against the wall of the mission station, seeking shelter from the sun on the cool side of low rocks that cast shadows not more than a few inches in length. The goats littered the village like crumpled pieces of newspaper.

We walked round a fat, tawny-coloured sow that lay with her large litter in the middle of the road.

"Are you going?" Japie Krige asked me. "I could come with you. If you thought I wouldn't be in the way, that is."

The silence of early afternoon lay over the village and over the veld. From a great distance there came the sound of a piccanin's voice – a herd-boy calling his cattle. That sound seemed part of, and blended integrally with, the stillness.

"I don't know whether I should go," I answered after an interval of thought. "I really don't know."

The sandy road before us shimmered in the heat.

Fragments of bottle glass on an ant-hill flung back the sun's rays with a brilliance as piercing as the edges of the shards themselves.

"I don't mean, in order to go and *collect* anything," Japie Krige went on, sounding half apologetic. "I am just thinking that – well, you know, when it's a case of somebody's death – the death of a close friend – well, you feel you want to do something, don't you? I don't suggest that you should go there just to fetch away his watch, say, as a keepsake."

Japie Krige made that last remark, I knew, in order to give a sardonic twist to his words. Like many people with a true warmth of feeling, he drew back from the idea of appearing sentimental.

I picked up a piece of rusted barbed wire and flung it a good distance into the veld. Lying where it had done, on the road, that barbed wire was a menace to the tyres of any motor vehicle passing that way. Not that that road *was* much used, of course, by any form of mechanical transport.

"Willem Lemmer did have a watch," I said to Japie Krige, "an old-fashioned gold watch with a chain and with enamel painting on the case. The watch should be – "

It was a queer thing. Just on account of my having *thought* of a motor-car in connection with that length of barbed wire, the spell of the Bushveld village's early afternoon torpor seemed to get lifted from me. The certain knowledge that there *was* that outside world of civilisation and rush and power stations and materialistic progress and cigarette ends lying on pavements – all this freed me, for a while, from a hypnotic power whose true nature I understood only too well, and from whose horror I recoiled almost as unthinkingly as I yielded to its fascination. For the feelings that went with a walk along the road through a Bushveld native village, on a hot afternoon, formed, I knew, a part of those other, darker feelings, that held in them both lure and menace.

" – should be worth quite a good bit," I said to Japie Krige.

"I hope there aren't any snakes, here," Japie Krige said as we stood with our suitcases on the tracks of the railway siding and the train was slowly disappearing from view among the thorn-trees.

Japie Krige surveyed, with marked disfavour, the tangled growths – varying in hue from a diversity of greys to vivid greens – through which a footpath undulated from the side of the railway line. The footpath looked a good deal like a snake, too, I thought – like a brown mamba, even, twisting its way through the grass. I did not, however, mention that to Japie Krige.

There was no one to meet us at the siding. For we had not written to Willem Lemmer's widow that we were arriving. Still, the Lemmer farmhouse was not many miles distant. It was certainly fewer miles away than one would readily imagine, standing on the railway track and seeing to the east and west a low line of koppies that looked all the more desolate for their intermittent covering of bush, and with the northern and southern horizons hidden from view by the immediate trees.

"If they didn't have those koppies, there," Japie Krige said, unconsciously speaking as though he were in a city and the koppies were buildings erected by human agency, "then it wouldn't feel quite so lonely. It would be bad enough, I mean. But if you had around you just bush, then you could imagine that there is nothing but bush anywhere. But with koppies, there, you can *see* that there is in the whole world nothing but bush."

Japie Krige did not sound very cheerful. He grew even more discouraged when I informed him that those koppies were the 'Nwatis. He remembered what I had told him about how unhealthy the area was. At the same time I said to him that, if he was really afraid of snakes, we could quit the footpath and take the wagon-road to the Lemmer farm, instead. Only, it was a longer way round. But Japie said, no, we could stick to the footpath.

He said he felt there were worse things in the folds of the 'Nwati hills than snakes. I did not think it necessary to tell him how right he was.

What was singular about my own feelings, I found, was that, having once decided to come there, the misgivings that obsessed my mind during that afternoon walk through the native village of Gouspoort were of a sudden dissipated. Even though there was now no more turning back, I felt almost buoyant – even though the way I had to tread was now narrowed to a footpath.

And the fact was that I was not now much concerned with how I myself felt about things. I was far more interested in Japie Krige's reactions. I could not help but reflect how much they had in common with my own feelings of a former time when I had carried a suitcase down that winding footpath, in the company of a man who had a letter that was similar to the letter folded in my breast-pocket now.

For some distance the way skirted a barbed-wire fence. On one side was the bush, on the other the stubble of a mealie land.

A number of natives were at work in the clearing – hard at work, too, by the look of it.

I drew Japie Krige's attention to this circumstance.

"That's one thing about Willem Lemmer's widow," I said to Japie. "She doesn't let tragedy overwhelm her. You can see she's got things on this farm in hand, all right. You'd think that, with the boss dead, the natives would be taking it easy, sitting in front of their huts drinking beer. Or lying by a stream, smoking dagga. But from the quick way those darkies are a-moving this way and that, you'd never think that master is in the cold, cold ground."

Japie Krige looked at me in surprise.

"You know, Frans," he said, "the way you're talking, it seems as you've got no feelings about death."

I replied, trying to sound cryptic, that some day, some day, perhaps, he would find out. "Only, in that case," I added, "it will be after my time."

It was only when the footpath came to an end, and we emerged into the homestead clearing, with the farmhouse at the end of it, that my former trepidation returned. The day was almost over. From the kraal came shouted words and the clanking of milk-pails. I looked down. At my feet a belated ant was scurrying home from work. I found that I was noticing trivial things again. Once more my spirit was obsessed with a fear whose cause I knew, but whose nature I could not define. For it was a mixed emotion. Inextricably blended with terror was something that came near to exaltation – but it was exaltation of an unholy sort.

And it was then that Japie Krige took it into his head to become facetious. I attributed his change of mood to the relief occasioned to his mind by the sight, in the distance, of a farmhouse with smoke rising from the chimney, suggesting comfort and human cheer after a journey through miles of inhospitable bush. Another thing, too, I thought, was that Japie Krige was seeking to imitate my own somewhat unhappy attempt at a plaisanterie of earlier on. Only, when *I* spoke like that, I said to myself, it was still daylight.

"Not a bad-looking place," was what Japie Krige said. "Why don't you marry Willem Lemmer's widow? After all, you've come here for something to remind you of him. Well, his widow is something he's left behind."

It was on the tip of my tongue to ask Japie Krige why *he* didn't marry her. But I refrained. Perhaps he would yet, one day. After all, the African bush *was* getting into his blood.

By now it was quite dark. But the gloom could not entirely shroud a fenced-in area to our right, in which there were mounds. Not all of the mounds had headstones.

A dove cooed.

Some small creature of the night stirred in the dark grass near us.

It seemed to me that my voice sounded exactly as Willem Lemmer's voice had sounded on that first occasion on which he and I had come together to that front door. And now I used the same words that Willem Lemmer spoke then.

"I got your letter," I said to Stoffelina as she opened the door for us. I saw at once that she looked more beautiful than ever.

Veld Story

THERE is a fascination about old cemeteries of the kind that are dotted about the South African veld, family graveyards at the foot of koppies; small plots for burial grounds that were laid out during the past century, in the old days when amongst the harnesses and riems and trek-chains in the wagon-house, or by the side of the sacks of mealies in the grain shed there was always, on every farm, ready for use in emergency, a coffin.

One such old cemetery – a comparatively large one – is at Warmbaths, the headstones bearing dates going back to the 1840s. A number of Voortrekkers were buried there, not those who were leaders of any Treks, but obscure persons, men and women and children, whose memories have been obliterated with the erasing of their names and the dates of their birth and death from the headstones. And when you look at the little mounds of sun-bleached stones (do they search the veld specially for stones of the whiter sort when a mound is raised over a grave, or does the sun make the stones white with the years? – the sun and the rain?) then a century doesn't seem so very long, somehow.

They must lie lightly on a grave, the stones that have not sunk so very deeply into the earth at the end of a hundred years.

And what is of more particular interest to a passer-by is an old cemetery somewhere on a lonely part of the veld, grown with tangled grass and oleanders and shut in with a barbed-wire fence, the rusted strands put very close together – and all traces lost long ago of the following generations of that family that had laid its dead to rest in a piece of ground closed in with barbed wire that is corroded with half a century of rust.

Such a graveyard I came across at the weekend on a farm that is within easy reach of Johannesburg. The farm has changed hands a good number of times in recent years. The new owners, I found, did not know very much about the original family of Van Heerdens, whose names are engraved on the headstones of the cemetery.

There is still a stretch of rising ground in the neighbourhood that is known as Van Heerden's Bult. But nobody named Van Heerden has lived in those parts for as long as most people can recall.

I could not, of course, resist the temptation to climb over that fence. The oleander – selon's rose, it is called in the Marico – at one time the most popular flowering tree in certain parts of the country, because it is hardy and stands up well to drought conditions, had grown tall and shaggy, through not having been pruned (for how long, I wondered?) but the colour of its flowers toned in well with the yellow of the grass and the sunlight and the pallid yellow of the mood evoked by the surroundings, and the upper part of the grave-yard reposed in the cool of the oleander's shade.

At a place where the rusted wire had sagged slightly I climbed over into the enclosure.

From force of custom I looked first at the jars that had once held flowers. As always, in a graveyard on the veld, there were a number of vases and urns, of glass and porcelain, that held a peculiar fascination because they belonged to the irrevocable past.

I have seen, on veld graveyards in the Transvaal, cut-glass vases that must have come from stately Cape homes; ornamental earthen-ware vessels graceful in shape and lovely in their colouring and of a quality and craftsmanship that has enabled them to remain, after half a century of weathering, still without crack or blemish.

It is also a not unusual circumstance to come across, in these iso-lated burial-places, bottles of antique design, some of them black and with short necks and heavy-bellied, as though they had once contained some potent liquor, others delicately shaped and in varie-gated patterns – made in far-off days to be receptacles of perfumes and unguents.

There were several interesting vases in this cemetery under the oleander. There was also a green bowl of cut glass, designed to hold fruit rather than flowers, exquisitely shaped and fitted with delicate silver handles. It had no doubt graced the sideboard of a dining room some three-quarters of a century before. The green bowl was in superb condition, almost as though the mud with which it had been periodically spattered by one rain to be washed off by the next had also served to polish the smooth external surfaces, lingering a while in the inner curves.

On another mound were two Dresden figurines, hollowed out at the top for flowers. One of the figures was slightly chipped, but it looked good for another couple of centuries.

The names on the tombstones were all Van Heerdens, or women with other surnames who had been born Van Heerden. I looked at the dates. The last interments had taken place in the early years of the present century. It must have been after that date that the Van Heerden family had trekked away.

Then I noticed a singular circumstance. The last six or seven tombstones all bore that same date, that year in the early part of this century. They were all Van Heerdens. And they had all been buried between the 14th and the 30th days of September. Seven members of the same family had all died within the same fortnight. The names and dates were still clearly legible. I made a closer study of the inscriptions. There were six children, three girls and three boys, the youngest eight, the oldest nineteen. And also the mother. At intervals from each other of a day or two a whole family had died and had been buried. During the month of September in a year in the early part of this century.

I wondered what had happened. How had they all come to die? It must have caused a stir in these parts, many years ago, an entire family dying out like that, within so short a period of time. It was something that must still be talked about, on winter's evenings when, the day's work done, people sat around the open fireplace in the kitchen and talked of strange things.

I went from one farm to the next to find out how it had all happened. And eventually I came across an old woman who had been born on a farm near where the Van Heerdens had lived. And as a young woman, who was then on the point of being married, she had attended the funerals of several of the children and of the mother. And this woman told me, simply, that the whole family had died of enteric. That was all there was to it. Just a simple story of the veld. And after that the father had trekked away. To Rustenburg, some said.

I thought, when I went away, what a wonderful theme the story of the deaths of the Van Heerdens could furnish for a novel. Each of these children and the mother. The little girl of fourteen on the threshold of womanhood, arrived at an age where she would furtively examine herself in the mirror, sloping the looking-glass downwards. And the young man of nineteen, who had passed through the sturm and drang of adolescence – something that would not happen to a city-bred youth for another ten years – and was already beginning to assume the responsibilities of manhood. And so with the rest of the family, with their problems and conflicts and frustrations. . . the dreams and griefs and bitterness of childhood, and the dark strugglings of adolescence. And I feel that Mrs Van Heerden was in many ways a remarkable woman. And then all these problems suddenly solved. Just when the stage is set for the development of character, for the unwrapping of the future, for the intricacies of the unfolding of the lives of all these people – suddenly, it all stops. The story is ended before it has begun. The problems are all solved before they have been fairly stated. All the loose ends tied up before they have become properly unravelled. Only life can create a story like that, so tremendous in its sweep, so intriguing in its possibilities – and so simple in the telling.

On the way back I repassed the graveyard. I also found the place where I judged the Van Heerden homestead had been. And some distance away was a spring, choked with gaudily coloured weeds and long thick grass of a brilliant green. A donga dense with all sorts of vegetation, blue lobelia and river reeds and rushes and kweekgras and yellow gazanias. And in this muddy water, slowly flowing towards the dam where there are wild ducks, must have been bred the enteric germ which half a century ago caused seven new mounds to be raised in the barbed-wire enclosure besides the unpruned oleander.

Red and pink buphane also grows by the side of the donga that leads from the spring to the dam.

86

The Old Muzzle-loader

I always attracted a considerable amount of attention, the flintlock Ou-Sanna that Gerrit Buys kept in the corner of his voorkamer, the gun standing upright in the rack that Gerrit had constructed out of tamboetie wood. The flintlock was about four feet high, overtopping by a good deal the little Portuguese Mauser placed in the adjoining compartment in the rack. The barrel of the Ou-Sanna was, of course, smooth. It was also wide, to accommodate the four ounces of lead that the gun had been wont to discharge, in the old days, to an effective distance of several hundred yards.

A caller at Gerrit Buys's farmhouse would, after a while – sometimes still holding the coffee-cup in one hand – get up from the stool or riempies bench on which he had been seated and gravitate in the direction of the gun rack. He would find himself led almost unconsciously into that corner. The Ou-Sanna was, for the Boer, a relic of national and sentimental and historic interest. The flintlock had played a dominant role in the opening up of the Orange Free State and the Transvaal to white settlement. And so a visitor to the home of Gerrit Buys would find himself ere long standing before that antique fire-arm from whose muzzle, silent now, the rounded lead had thundered long ago.

The smoke from the Ou-Sannas had hung about the wagons that rolled northwards with spans of Afrikaner oxen like red threaded beads. Above the wagons the gun-smoke was a blue wreath.

It was with such feelings, of pride in the old days when the Boer with his muzzle-loader was a power in the land, that the visitor would lift the Ou-Sanna from the rack in Gerrit Buys's voorkamer and with the barrel pointed downwards towards the earth floor would pull back the hammer, to release it to the accompaniment of a sharp click and a shower of sparks. Gerrit Buys kept the trigger mechanism of the Ou-Sanna oiled, for show. And so the hammer would strike against the flint, click-click, sending sparks into the now empty priming-pan.

There seemed something unnatural about the fact that with all this the gun did not thunder out a charge of lead shot. The old muzzle-loader seemed almost frighteningly silent.

Louis Wassenaar

W HEN the Voortrekkers first made their way in their ox-wagons through the stony region of the Witwatersrand, they didn't have dust from the minedumps blowing in under their wagon-tents.

Louis Wassenaar walked down Plein Street from the environs of the Drill Hall, in the direction of the Technical College, which he had known years ago as an annexe to the Witwatersrand University, of which only part of the main building, and the geological and zoological laboratories, had been completed when he first became a Witwatersrand University student. And all that was many years ago.

Today the Technical College was housed in that building at the main portals of which two men cast in concrete stood holding up the top floors of the edifice. Those men had been standing there for many years, also, never appearing to tire much. Louis Wassenaar remember-ed that as a child those two figures in stone had captivated his imagination. They had represented for him part of the essential reality of Johannesburg. And he remembered that, on one occasion, a dissolute uncle of his, who was known to the family as Oom Egbert, had inform-ed him that those stone men were taken down from their perch every five years. And in response to the enquiry of the small boy, Louis Was-senaar, as to why this was done ("What do they take those men down for, Oom Egbert?"), a reply was forthcoming that appeared humorous only in terms of adult conceptions of life. To the small boy, Louis Was-senaar, it was only a humane act, taking those men down at intervals so that they could exercise a certain natural function.

These, and other matters, occupied Louis Wassenaar's thoughts on this hot afternoon in the early summer, when he had passed the Union Grounds and the Elgin Hotel, and was walking down Plein Street in the direction of Eloff Street.

He passed a number of furniture shops and a fried fish establishment. And he was still thinking of the building that was today known as the Technical College. It was better in the old days. Then that building still formed part of the Witwatersrand University, with the Tin Temple at the back. T. J. Haarhoff was Professor of Latin; A. I. Wagner, now deceased was Senior Lecturer in Classics. And there was Professor Drennan English. And Jan Hofmeyr, now a Cabinet Minister, was on the point of relinquishing his job as Principal of Wits. And there was that limerick that a student – Pinchuck, his name was – had made up about T. J. Haarhoff, "who lived not far from the bar off", ending up with "and tum-titty – fell from the car off." And tum-titty. What were the words that fitted in there? Tum-titty. A dactyl. Ah, well, nobody would ever know. Least of all the student who composed that limerick. What had happened to Pinchuck, anyway? Louis Wassenaar suddenly remembered that he hadn't heard of or seen his former fellow student for years.

And that building had now been converted into the Witwatersrand Technical College. It was queer that he still had some sort of link with the place, Louis Wassenaar reflected. He didn't know any more of the lecturers there, of course. Or the professors, either – if you could call a man who taught in a technical college a professor. There was something in Louis Wassenaar's mind (that was saturated, in spite of himself, with certain academic prejudices), that rebelled at the idea. You couldn't have the Head of a Faculty, a Chair, a Dean, a Vice-Chancellor, at a technical college. Or could you? Louis Wassenaar had to admit that he didn't know for sure.

Louis Wassenaar's link with the present-day technical college lay in the circumstance of his being acquainted with a number of students in the art department. They were mostly youngsters, these art students, and Louis Wassenaar was not much impressed with the standard of their work. They did not to his mind reveal very much originality. They seemed considerably less talented than art students of their own age that he had come across in Paris and Brussels, and in Chelsea and Hampstead, even. And yet Louis Wassenaar was mildly interested in several of these students, somehow. He felt sure that his interest had nothing to do with the students themselves. They were all years younger than he was, for one thing. And several of them had the arrogance that comes from ignorance of life and a lack of knowledge of both the spirit and the technique of painting. But, of course, that was the thing that captured his interest, that last word, painting. The thought of colours flung on to canvas held a strong lure for Louis Wassenaar and the mere fact that these young art students, men and women, slapped paint about appealed to Louis Wassenaar's imagination.

And he wasn't always able to analyse his reactions. He couldn't always see clearly that art was one thing, a thing of truth and beauty and enduring magic, and that these young students who professed to practise art had really nothing very much to do with the eternal verities as understood and expressed by Van Gogh and Daumier. Because the word, art, had for Louis Wassenaar an immortal ring, he couldn't see clearly, always, that these students didn't have very much of a share in that heritage that is bound up with the immortalities.

Louis Wassenaar got to the intersection of Plein Street and Eloff Street. Before turning the corner down Eloff Street he took one more look at that building that was now the Witwatersrand Technical College, and that had once been the School of Mines and that had housed, in between, some of the lecture theatres of the Witwatersrand University. And during all those years those two naked men, hewn out of stone, had remained standing on each side of the doorway, holding up part of the building. These two were real men, living characters. And the men Louis Wassenaar remembered from Wits were real men, also, in the sense of their being characters who existed in actual life. Hofmeyr, the Principal, and those professors and lecturers. And some of the students: Zwarenstein and Benny Sachs and I. A. Maisels, and somebody called Wright, and a person who won the Rhodes scholarship once – what was his name? And Tick Davis. And Bunny Auret. And Sybil, somebody. What had happened to them all, anyway?

Those were the last real names and the last real people that came into Louis Wassenaar's mind. He turned down Eloff Street, down towards Cleghorn's, and from then onwards the things that happened and the people he met were all fiction.

Up to that moment of his turning the corner into Eloff Street everything was factual. Thereafter fiction came marching in with the flying of banners. Louis Wassenaar's turning into Eloff Street was like the entry into Phrygia of the hero of Apuleius's *Golden Ass*. Once you crossed the border into Phrygia you were no longer in the real world. Magic ruled. The most improbable things happened and seemed to be an integral part of everyday existence. The factual life that men lead had ceased to be, and the more intense and the more real life of fiction flung wide its coloured portals.

Gris Aniescu, born in Rumania and now a citizen of South Africa, stood on the crowded platform of one of those more old-fashioned trams that are in the service of the Johannesburg Municipal Department of Transport. Gris Aniescu was not standing on the platform of one of those amusing native trams, painted silver around the belly, or on the platform of one of those long, closed-in, streamlined looking

90

things. It was one of those shortish trams that let a lot of fresh air in and that have straps all the way down the sides, not for hanging on to but for pulling down when you want to stop the tram.

Gris Aniescu had been resident in Johannesburg for a good number of years. But he had not been in the city very long before he had detected the advantage of the old-fashioned type of tram. You could stand on the platform, well back, holding on to one of the uprights supporting the staircase, and from that position you commanded a good view of the legs of the girls and women descending the stairs. When the tram stopped at the Joubert Park gates quite a number of people descended the stairs from the upper deck. Mostly these passengers were men, in flannels or lounge suits. And a couple of soldiers in khaki shorts. Gris Aniescu glanced at their legs in disgust. There were also some school-girls, in blazers and gym-frocks. Gris Aniescu, student of legs, was not much interested in them, either.

In the next moment there swam before the gaze of Gris Aniescu a vision that took his breath away. A girl neatly shod in red shoes and wearing stockings of a sheer texture that did not have any of that cheap shine on them and that clung like breath on a window-pane, smoothly and intimately and very lightly, to a pair of dainty ankles and shapely calves – rounded enough just to be exhilarating – and two knees that seemed just the perfection of form and size and that seemed to have dimples in them. There was the billowing of an organdie frock, yellow as the summer in Johannesburg and as wide as the summer, and the next thing Gris Aniescu knew was that he was standing aside from the foot of the staircase, elbowing some of his fellow passengers in the ribs, in order to make way for this nymph in yellow organdie whose lower limbs had come out of the dreams of his adolescence and young manhood.

He never saw the girl's face. He wasn't interested in her face. But he would know those legs again anywhere. The yellow organdie frock alighted from the tram, gracefully, in a velvety sway of motion, moving like a perfumed wave, like the soft wind, as she must do, of necessity, Gris Aniescu reflected. With legs like that.

The organdie frock stepped on to the pavement and seemed to be making for the park gates. Gris Aniescu was in two minds as to whether to jump off the tram, which was already moving away again, and to follow those legs through the park. But the conductor's voice brought him out of the dream that was beating at his temples. The memory of those legs remained before his eyes as swift pulsations, coming and going, appearing and vanishing, vivid sensations that had an unearthly brightness in the throbbing of his blood.

"Plenty of room upstairs," the conductor announced.

Gris Aniescu was startled. It seemed to him almost, in terms of some sort of esoteric symbolism, that what the conductor was saying had direct reference to his own thoughts. . .

Ah, well, there was no harm in going upstairs, now, Gris Aniescu decided. To remain on the platform and wait for more girls to come down would be in the nature of anti-climax. He knew he wouldn't see a pair of legs like those again for a long time.

It was an Eloff Street tram. He would get off where the tram turned the corner into Market Street. And he would go round the corner from there into the Carlton bar for a couple of brandies. Those legs encased in sheer stockings had shaken him. He also remembered how straight the seams of the stockings at the back of the legs were.

At the corner where the tram turned, half a block from the Carlton, Gris Aniescu alighted. And so he ran into Louis Wassenaar who had reached as far as Market Street in his walk down to his office.

Shortly before he had turned into Eloff Street, where he had entered into the realm of fiction, Louis Wassenaar had been grappling, at odd intervals in between vaguely nostalgic thinking, with a problem. He wanted to write a story. He couldn't think of a plot. He wanted to write He couldn't think about what. It was an old problem. And there was never any simple solution to it.

Louis Wassenaar had himself assisted, some time in the past, a man who had got a contract from a correspondence school for compiling a series of postal lectures on the art of writing short stories. The man, incidentally, was Gris Aniescu. So peculiar a thing is life.

Before coming to South Africa, Gris Aniescu, emigrating from his native Bucharest, had knocked about the Western European continent a bit, in sundry obscure capacities, in the course of which he had acquired a working knowledge of a number of languages. He had learnt French, he explained, in Berlin, from a French prostitute resident in the then German capital. German he had learnt in the same somewhat irregular fashion in Paris. He didn't know any Russian: probably on account of the fact that he had not met a Russian prostitute during his period of residence in London.

When he arrived in South Africa, Gris Aniescu found himself at a loose end. He found that the fact of his having lived in places like Tottenham Court Road and the Chaussée de Wavre and the Avenue Louise gave him some sort of prestige with near-art circles in Johannesburg. The fact, also, that he could consume sizeable quantities of raw spirits without getting very noticeably drunk also served to stand him in good stead.

He had begun by giving lessons in foreign languages, notably French and German, thereby succeeding, incidentally, in greatly improving his English, so that in the end the accent of Tottenham Court Road was hardly to be detected in his utterance. Gris Aniescu had made quite strenuous efforts, also, to obtain pupils in Rumanian. But there seemed a peculiar dearth, in Johannesburg, of men and women anxious to learn his native tongue.

After a while, Gris Aniescu began branching out into one or two of the less generally recognised branches of freelance journalism. His English wasn't much worse than Michael Arlen's or Conrad's, but there were certain difficulties of syntax and idiom that he was never really able to overcome. For this reason, when he had been commissioned to turn out a series of articles or lectures or treatises on some unfamiliar subject – which the less enlightened Johannesburg editors thought he must know something about, merely because he had been in Bucharest and Paris and Berlin (before the war, of course) – then it was his practice to seek the assistance of some working journalist in Johannesburg to sub the stuff he had written. That was how he had first made contact with Louis Wassenaar, who was employed on the editorial staff of a somewhat obscure Johannesburg weekly magazine that was nominally concerned with cultural matters.

Now, as he strolled down Eloff Street, Louis Wassenaar tried to remember some of the stuff that went into that series of lectures on How to Write a Short Story, which Gris Aniescu had compiled for the correspondence college. Louis Wassenaar felt that he would be ethically justified in drawing on that source of knowledge and inspiration. After all, not only had he gone through all Gris Aniescu's manuscripts, improving the style and correcting the grammar, but he had also made many constructive suggestions in regard to both the form and content of these lectures. And his contribution to the lesson on How to Construct a Plot was, as Gris Aniescu had himself acknowledged, "significant."

Before he had got to Jeppe Street, Louis Wassenaar recalled some of the salient points in the lecture on How to Construct a Plot. There was first some reference to Shakespeare, in this lecture, it having been pointed out that Shakespeare hardly ever bothered to invent a plot, but just pinched whatever lay nearest to hand. The student was strongly advised against this course. Times had changed since the Elizabethan era. There was the Copyright Law. And modern editors frowned at literary theft, muttering darkly about that heinous sin known as plagiarism. It didn't do to steal plots any more – although all the Best Writers still did it, of course.

Louis Wassenaar remembered the next paragraph in that lecture: "You want to write a story. Has it ever occurred to you that the most entrancing situations in fiction are derived from the raw actuality of life itself? And then when you are racking your brains for an out-of-the-way theme, there is all the time the material for a first-class story lying right next to hand? Have you ever thought of writing a story about the situation in which you are actually finding yourself at this very moment? Have you thought of writing a story about an author who can't think of a plot? Try it."

Louis Wassenaar smiled wryly. What junk that was to palm off on to young and ambitious writers, anyway. And it was not only dud advice. It was also most unoriginal. He had the feeling at the back of his mind that he had read the same sort of advice in text-books on Freelance Journalism and Journalism as a Career and Learning to be a Writer. All that sort of baloney. Shakespeare had never been privileged to read works of that nature, or to take up a correspondence course in writing. And so Shakespeare just pinched his plots at random. No wonder the French classed Shakespeare as a barbarian.

"Take your stories from raw life." That sounded all right. There seemed a bit of sense in that. And what would be more raw than the life about him, here in the street, here, where he was standing on the crowded pavement on this hot summer's afternoon, waiting for the robot to change from red to green? Perhaps if he listened to the scraps of conversation from passing pedestrians he might overhear a phrase or two that would give him the idea for a story. Louis Wassenaar decided that he might even offer this suggestion to Gris Aniescu for incorporation in any future series of lectures on the art of short story writing which he might get commissioned to turn out.

Meanwhile, Louis Wassenaar pricked up his ears. Stray snatches of talk made contact with his tympanum.

"I like those brown shoes," one woman said to another, pushing her finger against a plate-glass window. "Made of imported calf, it says."

He couldn't do very much with that, Louis Wassenaar felt.

"Van pool tot pool is dit sewe duisend nege honderd – " a Helpmekaar student to another. No, Louis Wassenaar decided, there wasn't much inspiration for a short story in the Junior Certificate examination. (With the Matric it might perhaps have been different.)

"Have a heart, man, it's going on for half-past two." Louis Wassenaar consulted his watch. It was nearer a quarter to three. No, there wasn't much in that bit of talk, either – except that the soldier who had uttered these words, and who was leaning rather heavily on the shoulder of a civilian with a scarred face, appeared to be drunk.

"Abafzi 'nkulu le tshefu – " Not much of a lead in that, either. Louis Wassenaar didn't know any of the Bantu languages.

But suddenly, as though from nowhere, there occurred to Louis Wassenaar's mind a couple of clichés that he felt he must get Gris Aniescu to include in any fresh series of lectures he might be drawing up on Journalism as a Career. One of these well-rubbed phrases was "as full of meat as an egg." The other was "short stories, articles, sketches, comic verse, even – all is grist to the mill."

Louis Wassenaar chuckled. How did he happen to have forgotten those hardy old stand-bys in the first instance?

And it was at that very moment – for so singular is the pattern out of which the stuff of life is woven – that Gris Aniescu, alighting from the tram as it came to a stop in front of the kosher restaurant near the corner of Market Street, ran into Louis Wassenaar.

The two men exchanged greetings. Back-slapping, swear-words and all that. Just as though they hadn't seen each other only last week, and as though they weren't running into each other regularly, in pubs, drawing-rooms, on street-corners and at parties.

Louis Wassenaar saw before him a man neatly dressed in a dark suit, rather tall and not unhandsome and sporting a little black beard; he was aged about thirty-five. Half an inch or so of white shirt-cuff protruded from his coat-sleeves. Gris Aniescu thought that he looked distingué. In actual fact, if you knew a little about life, and you saw Gris Aniescu anywhere, on the Prado or near the Gare St Lazare or in Piccadilly or in Pritchard Street, you would recognise him as a second-rate battler.

"Will you come with me for a drink?" Gris Aniescu asked. "I have for you news."

(How would it be to start off a story with those words, Louis Wassenaar wondered? – "Will you come for a drink? I have for you news." – Once again he shook his head. Louis Wassenaar felt that in that opening there lay no possibilities at all.)

"I have to get back to the office," Louis Wassenaar replied to Gris Aniescu. "I don't know how on earth I am ever going to get through my work this week. The way it has accumulated. Art exhibitions. Topical comments. Write-ups for advertisers. Thousands and thousands of words. I don't know where to start. But I'll come and have a quick one with you."

Gris Aniescu led the way across the street and in at the front entrance of the Carlton Hotel.

"No good, Gris," Louis Wassenaar called out. "I've told you I've got work to do. If we go upstairs to the lounge we'll sit down and start chatting, and we won't get out of there for another hour. Let's go through into the lounge bar. It's got to be a quick one."

"What's yours?" Gris Aniescu enquired, when they were leaning up against the counter that was like an oval island afloat on a vast sea of thirst. Was there any time of the day or night when this pub was not crowded? Louis Wassenaar couldn't be sure.

The bartender put their brandies before the two men.

Gris Aniescu started feeling in his pockets. Louis Wassenaar took out his wallet, from which he extracted a note.

"No, no," Gris Aniescu declared. "It is my treat. It is I who have invited you."

By the time Gris Aniescu had produced half a crown from his pocket the bartender had already taken Louis Wassenaar's note and was changing it at the cash register.

"The next one," Gris Aniescu said, earnestly, "will have to be mine."

"There won't be a next one," Louis Wassenaar replied. "I have work waiting for me. What was that news you had for me? Is it a story, perhaps? I am trying to get hold of a plot for a story."

"What I have to impart to you," Gris Aniescu announced, " is of far greater significance. In the tram from Twist Street coming down I saw today the most beautiful girl in the world. But beautiful."

He paused to allow the other man to assimilate the full emotional content of this word.

"But beautiful," Gris Aniescu went on, putting his fingers to his lips and blowing a kiss in the direction that seemed most remote from the company of male bar-loungers hanging on to the edge of the counter. "She is a perfect subject for a great artist, for the greatest portrait painter of all time. I shall know her again wherever in the world I see her at any time once more."

"Is she dark or fair?" Louis Wassenaar enquired, mildly interested.

Gris Aniescu thought for a few moments. The shape of those legs under the yellow frock. A mass of yellow billowing over those clean and aesthetic and yet warmly insinuating curves. Those legs – oh, clearly, they had brunette curves.

"She is dark," Gris Aniescu announced. "Yes, quite definitely, and she is – " working out the rest of the details of her anatomy from what he had seen of her legs as they came down the stairs – "she is tall, but not too tall, and she is inclined slightly on the slender side, and she has a white forehead and straight eyebrows, I think: no, no, her eyebrows they are bent just like that" – he drew a line on the counter with a forefinger dipped in brandy – "and she has the most gentle nature, the most sweet and loving disposition in the world. What a subject for a portrait painter!"

"But how could you tell all that just by looking at her?" Louis Wassenaar demanded. "Her character and her disposition and all that?"

"I looked at her, of course," Gris Aniescu replied. "I looked at her legs. As she came down the stairs. I never saw her face. There was no need. I never saw her face at all. Just her legs. That was enough. Her legs, they told me all."

Louis Wassenaar pondered a moment, in faint mystification.

"But, dash it all, man," he said. "You've just told me that she would be an ideal model for a portrait painter. And now you say you haven't even seen her face."

"Her legs," Gris Aniescu insisted. "From her legs I know everything about her. Everything."

Before they knew where they were they had ordered another round of brandies. This time, in the juggling that went on for loose change, Gris Aniescu produced his half-crown only a fraction of a second after Louis Wassenaar had placed the payment for the two drinks in the bartender's hand. Gris Aniescu was improving. He was getting quicker at producing that half-crown.

Meanwhile, Louis Wassenaar was weighing up Gris Aniescu's reactions to that girl's legs, trying to get an angle on it, wondering how he could work it up into a theme for a short story. But it wouldn't go,

Louis Wassenaar decided. Any reader would spot right away that it was just some of Gris Aniescu's blah.

"The colour of your tram-cars," Gris Aniescu was saying. "Such a horrid colour of red. I am ashamed each time when I step on to the tram, and I was ashamed to look back at that girl. I did not want that she should have a recollection of me thus, standing on the platform of a red-painted tram-car. Now, if it was of a blue – not of the blue of a sky, but of a mysticism. Like the Egyptians spoke of it as to be blue when you stood in the temple before the altar in the ecstasy religious. Now, if in Johannesburg they had only the blue tram-cars. Then there would not be this barbarity. This Philistinism. There would not be these dreadful art exhibitions. The artistic spirit of a lover of the beautiful who comes from Paris here would not be offended, no more, by the gross taste the people of Johannesburg display in the furnishings of their homes. An Egyptian altar blue, now, for the painting of the tram-cars. The people of Johannesburg would learn – perhaps if I suggest it to the mayor I will get rewarded for it, no? Perhaps a thousand pounds. Perhaps two thousand pounds. But what is money? I do not care for their two thousand, maybe, even, three thousand pounds."

Only because his voice got slightly heavier was it possible to detect that Gris Aniescu was busy drinking. That was after the third brandy, for which Louis Wassenaar had paid again. Gris Aniescu had given up juggling with that half-crown.

Louis Wassenaar was not in as good shape as his friend. Maybe it was the hot weather. But Louis Wassenaar was distinctly conscious of the fact that all was not well, in that pub. At the back of his mind there was the consciousness, somewhat less urgent, now, of the amount of work that was waiting for him in his office. And those men leaning on the counter of the oval bar seemed no longer to be floating on the waves of their thirst. They seemed to be drowning somewhat rapidly. It was as though the edge of the bar counter was the shining beach of an island that these storm-tossed, shipwrecked mariners had reached – and that they had been washed up on shore a few hours too late. Louis Wassenaar shook his head vigorously. He must get rid of these thoughts. He didn't want to get drunk.

Look at those two men, there, for instance, standing there near the beer-pump. They were looking at him suspiciously. It was a bad sign when you thought strangers were looking at you with suspicion. But were they strangers? He wasn't sure now. But he believed that he had seen them before, somewhere, that soldier who was hanging on to a short, broad-shouldered man who was dressed in a grey suit and whose face was scarred. Oh, of course, he remembered, now. He had seen them in Eloff Street. And they had spoken about the time. Now he realised why they were in a hurry. They had somewhere to get to. To this pub. Louis Wassenaar began wondering idly as to how much of this sort of thing there was in the world. People hurrying to get somewhere. And then that somewhere was a pub. That seemed a very profound thought.

But then, why were they looking at him? They didn't know him, that soldier and that scar-faced civilian. He hadn't discussed the time with them on his way down Eloff Street. Or had he? He couldn't remember for sure, now. He couldn't remember, either, how many brandies he had had. Or how that glass almost half full of brandy and water came to be in his hand at that moment. He thought he had just finished off a brandy. Somebody must have pushed that glass into his hand. This was getting bad. He must sober up. Perhaps he should talk to Gris Aniescu a bit. That would help him to get his faculties cleared, through his having to concentrate. He would tell Gris Aniescu about what he should write in his next series of lectures on Journalism. Those battered and weather-worn clichés he had thought of.

"Say, Gris," he said – and he was pleased to observe that that soldier and that civilian were no longer looking at him – "I have thought of something you left out of your lessons on How to Write for the Press. What does anybody want to write for the press for, anyway? Sounds like writing for a washing-mangle or that thing that they have going round and round in a laundry. If you must Write for the Press, why can't it be for a wine-press? It must be very nice to write for a wine-press. Your words will then all come out with thick purple sunshine on them. Your words will be like grapes and your thoughts will be like gold, rich with the splendid intoxication of the summer. Oh, yes, and what I wanted to say to you – are you listening, Gris?"

"I am always listening to my friend," Gris Aniescu replied. "And the bartender is listening if we want another drink."

Another somewhat flurried transaction was gone through and Louis Wassenaar went on talking.

"What I want to say to you, Gris," he explained, "is that you must write next time that it is as full of meat as an egg, and that everything is grist to the mill, ha, ha. You see the point? Everything is Gris to the mill. Funny, isn't it? It came out just like that."

"In Europe," Gris Aniescu announced earnestly, "we have what is called tone. You have no tone here in this country. I suppose the climate here in Africa is against tone. People's manners they are so bad here. They bump you in the street. Like that. Bump, bump. And they offer to stand you a drink in a bar when they don't know you at all. And in their actions so many people in Johannesburg are low – "

That was as far as Gris Aniescu got when a voice interrupted him. It was a deep, foreign-sounding voice. Louis Wassenaar was aware of the voice a good while, it seemed, before he became conscious of the speaker.

"Cheese that up now, with your lies, Schtroppski, you," the voice said to Gris Aniescu, who immediately turned round to confront the speaker. Louis Wassenaar turned round also. It was that short, scar-faced man in the grey suit; the soldier was still leaning heavily on his arm. So that was why the man had been staring, like that, Louis Wassenaar reflected. Because he knew Gris Aniescu. Louis Wassenaar felt relieved, all at once. It was good to realise that this man actually had been staring. He had feared that he was beginning to suffer from a persecution mania on top of his other complexes.

"Schtroppski," the scar-faced man said again, an ugly glint in his eye.

"I resent that," Gris Aniescu replied with cold dignity. "Schtroppski – that is not my name. I am Aniescu."

So that was it, Louis Wassenaar thought again. Schtroppski, whatever the word was, was a name. He had thought, the first time he heard the scar-faced man use it, that it was some Eastern European form of abuse.

"Schtroppski," the stranger repeated, belligerently, and then he said, "Shpertzikaloushtolomkal-ukrotsht Schtroppski."

Louis Wassenaar didn't know whether what had preceded the word Schtroppski was a Christian name with a lot of syllables or a recognised Cypriot opening gambit for a fight. As an Afrikaner, Louis Wassenaar felt that an expression like that was worth a punch in the eye, and he began to move forward slowly, only to be restrained by the soldier who had somehow let go his hold of the scar-faced man and had flung both arms around Louis Wassenaar's neck.

"Cheese it up," the scar-faced man said again, this time to the soldier, and then proceeded to address Gris Aniescu some more.

"Schtroppski," the scar-faced man announced – it was getting rather monotonous, Louis Wassenaar thought: didn't they have much of a voca-

100

bulary in the Balkans? – "When we was stayed in that room in Melk-thoi you steal my socks. My one pair brown sock. Say, come clean, guy, you – "

Bracing himself suddenly, Louis Wassenaar succeeded in disengaging the soldier's arms from around his neck and standing him up against the counter.

"Take your friend outside," Louis Wassenaar heard the bartender say. "I can't have drunks in here. I'll lose my licence."

"This soldier isn't a friend of mine," Louis Wassenaar answered. "It's the first time I've seen him. No, I mean it's the second time. The first time was in Eloff Street."

Louis Wassenaar was glad to realise that he was sobering up. All that was left now was to get Gris Aniescu out of the pub as well. Then he could get to his office and work. Only, the dispute about the socks was getting rather heated. He hoped it wasn't going to develop into a brawl.

"Perhaps you would wish to take in return for those socks, of which I remember nothing, the socks which now I have on my feet?" Louis Wassenaar heard Gris Aniescu ask of Scar-face, in tones of withering sarcasm. "Perhaps you desire that I should sit down here, on the stool by the counter, and remove my own socks from where I have them on my two feet, and deliver them up to you?"

Scar-face explained that that was exactly what he wanted. Nothing less.

The rest didn't take very long. The soldier got into the way once or twice. And a few of the bar-loungers paused for a moment or two, from their talking and their drinking, to watch the operation, which they appeared to regard as somewhat unusual. And when Gris Aniescu had got his shoes off, sitting on a high stool with his back to the bar counter, and was beginning to remove his socks, there was a certain amount of whistling and the bartender said "Phew." But it was all over quite soon. And, except for a hole in one heel, they seemed a fairly good pair of socks that Aniescu handed over to Scar-face, who thrust the socks into his jacket pocket with what might have been a grunt expressive of gratitude at having his stolen property restored after the interval of many years.

"Are those the same socks?" Louis Wassenaar enquired, when he and Gris Aniescu were out on the pavement again. "They look as though they could have been the same pair."

"That is what I always say about Johannesburg people," Gris Aniescu remarked, continuing from where he had left off (before the interruption of the socks incident), "they have not got what in Europe we know as tone – "

Louis Wassenaar went on to his office with his brain working warmly and rapidly. He sat in front of the typewriter in the throes of a strong creative urge.

Gris Aniescu had given him an idea for a story.

The Ox-riem

IT was in those days, when there was no such thing as a Society for the Prevention of Cruelty to Children in the Pilanesberg area – any more than there is today, of course – and the only redress a child had when it was being subjected to inhuman treatment at home was to go and lie in a donga and weep – that the farmers on the other side of the Dwarsberge began to comment, in a somewhat adverse fashion, on the treatment that was being meted out to the young girl, Marie van Zyl by her guardian, Stefanus Aucamp, the owner of the farm Maanfontein.

Stefanus Aucamp was a man in his early forties. He lived alone on his farm Maanfontein, in a house that had whitewashed walls and a thatched roof and that was built at the foot of a koppie, in a place where the tall withaaks had already given way to thorny scrub.

Stefanus Aucamp had never married. For twenty years a kaffir woman called Blouta and her husband, Kees, had looked after Baas Aucamp's house with the whitewashed walls, cooking the master's meals for him, growing vegetables in the garden between the kitchen and the dam, repairing the thatch when the roof leaked, applying a new coat of whitewash when the walls became discoloured.

It seemed to be only the outside of the house that Stefanus Aucamp cared about at all. What there was of furniture was mostly of tamboetie wood and handmade. A long unpolished table in the voorkamer, a number of chairs and a crudely constructed bench with riempies for the mat two huge chests in which dried seeds and articles of clothing were packed away almost indiscriminately. The cutlery was worn. The crock ery was chipped. It was only on rare occasions, at intervals of several years, sometimes, that Stefanus Aucamp would think of spending a few minutes in that hardware shop, when he was in Zeerust for the Nagmaal, in order to purchase a couple of soup-plates, or half a dozen cups and saucers, to replace those pieces which Blouta and her husband Kees had broken in the kitchen.

There were three bedrooms, one facing on to the front stoep with its slate floor, the other two at the back of the house. Stefanus Aucamp slept in the front room, on a double bed made out of thick bushveld timbers and a mat of plaited thongs to serve as springs. A couple of reebok skins lay on the stone floor. For the rest, there was a wash-stand with a cracked enamel basin and a table and a chair. A piece of curtaining was fastened crosswise in one corner. Behind this hung the store suit that Stefanus Aucamp had worn for the past ten years on each of his visits to the town of Zeerust at Nagmaal.

On a wall was a religious print, the surface considerably damaged by time and damp and the attentions of the white ants.

The furnishing in the other two rooms – one of which was today occupied by the girl-child, Marie van Zyl – was not substantially different from the room in which Stefanus Aucamp slept.

Stefanus Aucamp had had big ideas, at one time, people said. He had had large-scale plans for extending the house and getting the most modern kind of furniture, a chesterfield suite and wardrobes with mirrors and a dressing-table and a piano – all to be railed up from Johannesburg. He had spent a lot of time studying catalogues from furniture dealers. And the catalogues were very much discoloured from the grease on his broad, flat fingers, by the time that he decided that he was going to take no trouble with the interior decoration and furnishing of his house at all.

That was after a young woman in the Schweizer-Reneke District had written to say that she had decided, on thinking the matter over carefully, that she would not marry him. They say that Stefanus Aucamp changed a good deal, after he had received that letter, and that he had ceased taking any further interest in the furnishing of his house, and that he began, from then onwards, to devote all his time to the three thousand morgen of bush country that constituted his farm.

He cut down the trees and shrubbery on a stretch of level ground that was far removed from his homestead, and on this ground he began to sow corn, which was an unknown crop in that part of the country. He did a number of other unusual things as well, all of which were frowned upon by the farmers, at the beginning. But always, when a season or two had elapsed, it was noticed that most of the farmers followed in the footsteps of Stefanus Aucamp.

The only farmer who would not allow himself to be influenced by the innovations which he saw Stefanus Aucamp introducing was a near neighbour, Gawie Steyn.

They were much alike, Gawie Steyn and Stefanus Aucamp. That was after Stefanus Aucamp had got the letter from the girl in Schweizer-Reneke, and he had grown taciturn, almost overnight. And deep lines became suddenly cut in the corners of his mouth. And he would stand for long periods and stare in front of him, in silence, even when he was at a meeting of the Farmers' Association, and there were people present who spoke to him. Stefanus Aucamp and Gawie Steyn were much alike, after that. They were both long, sinewy men, for all the world like the shapes of men fashioned out of dried leather. They spoke little. Most of the time their thoughts seemed to be far away, where their eyes were. It was easy to understand why Stefanus Aucamp should have become like that. Brooding and morose, and speaking but few words. But it was a different thing with Gawie Steyn, who had a young wife, and several children, who would play around his knee in the evening, when the day's work on the farm was done, and he would sit on a riempies chair, in the gathering dusk, and the wind of the early evening would blow through the tall withaaks and the sound of children's voices would be in his ears. And yet Gawie Steyn would sit on his front stoep, smoking away at his pipe, and it would almost be as though he did not notice that his children were there. And he did not speak.

For a while there was a certain measure of life in the farmhouse at Maanfontein. That was when a bywoner and his wife and their daughter, who was then an infant, lived with Stefanus Aucamp in his house with the thatched roof and the whitewashed walls. They remained there for several years, the bywoner, Gert van Zyl, and his wife and their small daughter, Marie. But it did not appear to make much difference to Stefanus Aucamp's disposition, this circumstance of a family coming to live in his house. That air of moody silence never seemed to leave him. Nor did he appear to take much more interest in the domestic arrangements of the place. It was also said that the only time he had been known to quarrel with the bywoner family was on one occasion when Mrs Van Zyl had taken it on herself to order a quantity of household utensils from the store in Zeerust, in order to introduce a measure of rude comfort into the lives of the farmer of Maanfontein and his employee and family.

Then, one day, when the girl-child Marie, then aged about six years, had been left in the house, in the charge of the kaffir woman Blouta, and her parents had set off for Zeerust by mule-cart, to transact certain business for Stefanus Aucamp, there occurred a simple tragedy of the veld that resulted in the child, Marie, becoming an orphan, and in Stefanus Aucamp assuming the office of guardian of a girl of six whose nearest relatives, as far as was known, were a trekboer family who had more children than they could support.

What had happened was simply that Gert van Zyl and his wife, on their return from Zeerust, tried to cross the Molopo River when it was in flood (Gert van Zyl having apparently been drunk at the time), and that the mule-cart was swept downstream and the occupants drowned.

With the kaffir woman, Blouta, to look after her, Marie van Zyl went on staying on the farm Maanfontein. The education she received was sketchy. She attended a farm school eight miles away from Maanfontein for a number of years. She got to the school and back by mule-wagon, which passed near Maanfontein daily to convey the children from the neighbourhood to school. Afterwards, when the school wagon ceased passing near Maanfontein, because of the decline in the number of children in that area who attended school, Stefanus Aucamp kept Marie van Zyl at home. He said that he was not going to provide transport to enable a bywoner's child to get educated above her station.

It was about this time, too, that people began to comment on certain aspects of Stefanus Aucamp's treatment of the orphan girl, saying that the discipline he maintained erred grievously on the side of oversternness. That Stefanus Aucamp knew what was being said about him by the neighbours was not doubted. There was much talk about his conduct. People also hinted to him openly, and to his face, about the things that went on in their minds in regard to this matter.

This had no effect on Stefanus Aucamp. His manner of using the orphaned Marie van Zyl grew steadily more inhumane.

Long and tough and like dried leather, Stefanus Aucamp spent more and more time on the lands. The barbed wire that fenced in his farm and that divided it into a number of camps was tightly drawn. He experimented with a mixture of Stockholm tar and the powder of cattle-dip and other ingredients which he smeared on the lower parts of his fencing-poles to keep the white ants away. The other farmers at first ridiculed his experiments. Afterwards they came and asked him for the recipe. Sullenly, without any human warmth, but also without resentment, he would impart to them such information as they sought. Afterwards his neighbours would also consult him on other matters, such as his views on how long the keelvel of an Afrikaner bull ought to be. And although they affected to despise his opinions, they themselves being fully versed in such matters, which they had studied almost unconsciously from childhood, the raw things of the soil forming an intimate part of their very breath and being – nevertheless, Stefanus Aucamp's neighbours liked to hear his views, even if it was only in order that they might reject them.

They came and spoke to Stefanus Aucamp, even though he was a difficult man to talk to. He never conversed. He would wait a long time before he replied to a question. It was as though the question and his answer would go round and round in his brain, for a long time, and that what he had to say came out of much darkness, and so when he finally replied it was often in a single word. And there were many occasions when, no matter what was said to him, he did not reply at all.

The only man who did not consult Stefanus Aucamp on any matter was his nearest neighbour, Gawie Steyn, a man who was also taciturn, and long and leathery, and who would sit for long periods in the evening, on his front stoep, gazing out beyond the shadows that were suspended between the koppies, and who did not seem to hear the voices of his children playing about his knee.

What people thought was particularly unnatural in the way Stefanus Aucamp was beginning to treat the child Marie was the fact that from morning to night she was seen working in the fields. She would be sent out to search for strayed cattle, like a boy. She would work on the lands with a hoe, like a kaffir woman. When Stefanus Aucamp planted a large area with potatoes – or a crop which, for once, turned out a failure: the farmers had said that you couldn't grow potatoes in that soil, and Stefanus Aucamp had lost a considerable measure of prestige when the crop came to nothing – then Marie van Zyl worked on the land for day after day with the planting, following behind the plough with a basket of seed potatoes, helping to take turns, with the kaffirs, in thrusting the potatoes into the earth and covering up the furrows again.

By that time Marie van Zyl was about fourteen. Her hands were rough from working in the fields. She had had small opportunity of acquiring knowledge of the softer things of life, or the more womanly side of domesticity. And what people felt most bitter about, people who had children of their own and who knew that a child should not be spoilt, were the things that came to their ears of the merciless fashion in which Stefanus Aucamp thrashed the fourteen-year-old child, Marie van Zyl.

There was a riem of ox-leather hanging on the wall in the kitchen. With this riem Stefanus Aucamp was in the habit of thrashing the child for the most trivial of offences, or even for no reason at all. Sometimes Marie van Zyl would cower away in the corner, suffering Stefanus Aucamp's blows mutely. At other times she would scream and rush out of the door, and Stefanus Aucamp would go after her, thrashing her across her back with the riem as she ran.

Stefanus Aucamp would thrash this child like you would thrash a kaffir, people said. Like you would thrash a dog.

It was right that children should be properly brought up, that they should be trained in the ways of the Lord from their earliest years. The Bible said so. If you weren't disciplined in your childhood you grew up into a godless person. That much everyone knew. For that reason a child had to be chastised, to be instructed in godliness through the sternness of love.

But what went on there, on the farm Maanfontein, with Stefanus Aucamp running after the child Marie van Zyl and flaying her back open with that ox-riem was a different thing. It was very dreadful. And there was nothing that could be done about it.

When she was fifteen, getting to that age when she began to take an interest in herself and her appearance, Marie van Zyl came out of the kitchen door one Saturday, when it was almost noon, and she carried a soiled cotton frock under her arm.

Stefanus Aucamp was entering the kitchen door at that moment.

"Where are you going?" he demanded, looking sternly at the girl.

Marie van Zyl avoided his gaze.

"To the dam, Oom Stefanus," she answered. "I go to wash my frock for this evening. The Bekkers are fetching me to the debating society meeting in Dwarsvlei."

"Debating society!" Stefanus Aucamp thundered. "Next it will be a dance. Next they will want to make a harlot out of you. Throw drown that frock and start carrying manure to the lands."

Marie van Zyl hesitated for a few moments. The next thing she knew was that Stefanus Aucamp had walked into the kitchen and had returned with the length of ox-riem.

His face looked dreadful in that it was so totally expressionless. She felt his tall leanness rising up over her. Like the in-heat rearing up of an animal. His breathing, also, was like that of an animal.

The ox-riem bit into her flesh and she ran in the direction of the dam, Stefanus Aucamp following at her heels and striking at her flee-ing body, for some distance, until his fury had abated.

Marie van Zyl spent that afternoon, the whole of it, carrying sacks of manure from the kraal to the lands. She winced often, when the weight of the sack was not properly adjusted and a hard lump of ma-nure pressed through the hessian against a place on her back or shoul-der where her skin was raw from the impact of the ox-riem.

Stefanus Aucamp spoke to the girl Marie van Zyl but rarely. And what he had to say he conveyed in as few words as possible. And in his voice there was always the undertone of a bitterness that could not be slaked. But in those times when he thrashed the child with the length of ox-hide he did not speak at all. It was like a silent ritual of the earth, those motions gone through in the unbleached monotony of stripes laid on young flesh. And always after he had laid the ox-riem to Marie van Zyl's body Stefanus Aucamp would stride out into the veld, walking for a long while in silence, his footsteps solid on the brown ground, and heavy, as though part of the dry glebe-land and the dusty clods to which Stefanus Aucamp belonged.

But there was another side, also, to the life that surges out of the ploughed field, and to this side of that life Stefanus Aucamp did not be-long.

There was again a Saturday on which Stefanus Aucamp encountered Marie van Zyl at the kitchen door. She was once more on her way to the dam, with a cotton dress under her arm. And again Stefanus Aucamp had gone into the kitchen for the ox-riem, and he had driven her out on the mealie-lands, where there was work to be done. But this time, after Stefanus Aucamp had left her, his fury sated, and he had gone back into the kitchen, to restore the ox-riem to its place on the wall, Marie van Zyl had not stopped running. She ran through the mealie-fields and through the clearing beyond, and it was when she was clambering through the barbed-wire fence that separated Gawie Steyn's farm from Maanfontein, that Stefanus Aucamp guessed what was happening.

Stefanus Aucamp went to the stables and saddled his horse with the speed of frenzy. He whipped the animal into a furious gallop. Horse and rider tore through hedge and thorn-bush and cleared barbed-wire fences and grazed past enormous ant-hills.

But Marie van Zyl had had too much of a start. She rushed in at Gawie Steyn's front door a few moments before Stefanus Aucamp came galloping up the path to the farmhouse. He had by this time whipped the horse into a condition of near-madness. The animal was foam-flecked from a three-mile gallop. His barrel-shaped chest heaved in quick pants that seemed like a death agony. His eyes rolled as though in the last pains of torture.

It was at that moment that Gawie Steyn came to his front door. Marie van Zyl had already dashed into the voorkamer. Stefanus Aucamp was getting ready to dismount before his horse had come to a stop in front of the veranda.

Gawie Steyn stepped forward, his arms folded lightly across his chest. He looked Stefanus Aucamp straight in the eyes. With one foot already out of the stirrup, Stefanus Aucamp paused. He understood, then. Neither man spoke. In Gawie Steyn Stefanus Aucamp had found a man as taciturn as himself.

Stefanus Aucamp swung himself back into the saddle. He did not look back again. A moment later horse and rider were careering madly back in the direction from which they had come.

Marie van Zyl did not remain long on Gawie Steyn's farm. Perhaps it was that Gawie Steyn's wife did not welcome the presence in their home of a girl of fifteen, who was near grown to womanhood. Perhaps there were other reasons. At all events, the time came, and soon, when Marie van Zyl set off, on her own, to the city of Johannesburg, and nothing more was heard of her.

It was not unlikely that in the city Marie van Zyl found that her body, lithely rounded in youth, was worth more than it was on the farm. And that her golden hair could be displayed to better advantage against the background of a hotel lounge than it could be, in the old days, in close proximity to a sack of manure.

But the person one should be sorry for, of course, was Stefanus Aucamp, who had once before been disappointed in love, and who had seen a girl-child grow before his eyes into young womanhood, and who knew that he was too old for her, too slow of speech and long and leathery, like the ox-riem. He knew that she could never be his, that she would never look at him as a woman looks at a man.

And there were many nights, in the years that came after, when Stefanus Aucamp would be seated alone in the kitchen, before the big open grate, and nobody could guess what his thoughts were about. And the length of ox-riem would be hanging idle on the wall of the kitchen – the riem that had often curved in a salt caress about the thighs of the young girl, Marie van Zyl.

The foregoing little story – which Louis Wassenaar had entitled "The Ox-riem" – was the subject of discussion, now, between Louis Wassenaar and Mavis Smith. They were seated in the lounge of the Grand National. Louis Wassenaar had phoned Mavis Smith after he had completed the story, and so they met after work (as was their habit when Louis Wassenaar had anything of unusual interest to communicate), in the lounge of the Grand National Hotel.

Mavis Smith put down the manuscript. She had read the story through to the end. The story of Stefanus Aucamp and Marie van Zyl. And the strip of untanned ox-hide that had formed the romantic link between a man and a girl.

"That's all right," Mavis Smith was saying, "I see what you are trying to get at with this story. But what I don't understand is what you told me about it before I started reading the story. You know, you said to me that you got the idea for this story through what happened between Gris Aniescu and that other foreigner in the pub you were talking about. Perhaps I am getting drunk, I don't know. How many have we had, anyway?"

"Two," Louis Wassenaar lied. "Only two."

"Well," Mavis Smith continued, "what I am trying to get at is just this, that I don't see the point about how you could have got the idea for this story about the young girl Marie van Zyl and the long, middle-aged man, Stefanus Aucamp, and what happened on that backveld farm: how you could have got the idea out of that other Rumanian making poor old Gris Aniescu hand over his socks. I don't see the connection. It sounds homosexual, almost."

"Oh, I see," Louis Wassenaar answered. "You don't see how it came about that after what happened in the Carlton bar between Gris Aniescu and his compatriot – that it should follow naturally that when I got back to the office I should have sat down and written this story which I am calling 'The Ox-Riem'? You don't see the parallels, the underlying one-ness in the two stories? By the way, I wonder how it would be to call the story just 'Ox-Riem', leaving out the 'The' – or how it would sound calling it just 'Riem'? You know, I think it sounds good, just one word, like that. 'Riem.' Earthy. Stark. Raw life that is heavy with the soil. How do you like it, Mavis?"

"I suppose it is all right," Mavis Smith replied. "But I still don't see how it fits in with the incident at the Carlton. That's the only thing that's worrying me. If you had given me this manuscript to read, simply as a little backveld story – a psychological study – all right, I would have been able to form an opinion of it, on my own. I would have been able to feel about it a singleness of effect. I would have known how to react to the denouement of your story. But I can't, now. I have been worrying about it all the time, trying to trace the similarity in the plot to whatever is the leitmotif of Gris Aniescu's encounter in the pub with that other foreigner, who walked off with his socks. It's been worrying me. It's spoilt your story about this girl and man on the Bushveld farm, if you understand what I mean – "

Louis Wassenaar reflected for some time.

"No," he said, eventually. "No, I don't see your point. To me, the connection is clear enough. It's like this – "

And he started to explain. Mavis Smith continued to look dubious.

Kandora House is still there, at the lower end of Jeppe Street, just before Doornfontein starts.

This is a very old building, constructed on temporary lines, in the way they erected tenement houses in Johannesburg fifty years ago. Slum houses in Johannesburg today are of two kinds, places that were at one time stately mansions of the rich and that have since fallen into decay, cut up into rooms and flats and occupied by white and coloured and Indian families with hordes of scantily clad, sore-eyed children. In their squalor these buildings retain memories of a past when the pavements of Johannesburg were gaudy with romance, and in their high-ceilinged drawing rooms – now bug-ridden and partitioned off into congeries of bed-sitting-rooms – Johannesburg's gold-mining aristocracy of half a century before once entertained on a scale that was opulent in its display.

But Kandora House is not one of those buildings. Kandora House was built as a slum tenement. It was meant to house mostly men, miners and workmen who were trying to save up money to get married on, men who had come to the Golden City as adventurers and who were seeking some avenue through which to get to the top, and who were down-and-out and had to stay in a place like that until the tide of their fortunes turned. So this building has no memories of better days. And they haven't pulled it down yet.

But what Kandora House has done during the half-century of its existence as a double-storeyed tenement building has been to build up a tradition of its own. In this respect it has achieved something that a stately mansion of the past, now overtaken by slumdom, has not been able to. During the years it has created its own atmosphere of life and people and the thick substance of history. Out of the lives of people who have come and gone over the period of half a century Kandora House has made its own traditions. People who lived and hoped and dreamt and whored, and who found a stray fragment of beauty, now and again, suddenly, illumining thereby the squalor of their existences; and who thieved and smoked dagga and sold liquor illicitly to the natives in the back yard, and lusted and committed murder, and made women pregnant in the suffocating poverty of a foetid bedroom with an unpainted door opening on to a wooden veranda; and children were born there, and men and women died there; and criminals and prostitutes were arrested there.

A dilapidated double-storeyed slum tenement, that you enter through a grimy doorway, the floor of the stone passages downstairs slopped over with pools of greyish water, Kandora House has more life in it than any block of luxury flats that they aren't thinking of tearing down, yet, because Kandora House has got more tales to tell than a more respectable building.

And it was to Kandora House that Marie van Zyl had come, several years after she had run away from Gawie Steyn's farm. It must have been that she had done wrong, in the first place, in having deserted Stefanus Aucamp, the man who had driven her before him with the ox-riem. The fact remained that she did not stay very long in Gawie Steyn's house, either. This time it had been Gawie Steyn's wife who had been a factor making for Marie van Zyl's unhappiness. Gawie Steyn's wife did not conceal her jealousy of the fair-haired girl of fifteen who had come running into her voorkamer, one day, breathless for sanctuary. It was almost as though Gawie Steyn's wife knew more than the world guessed as to the reasons underlying her husband's long spells of moody silence. After a few years Marie van Zyl ran away from Gawie Steyn and his wife, also. And she went to Johannesburg.

But it was only many months afterwards that she drifted, late one evening, into the vile-smelling cesspool that Kandora House represents for people who reject the paramount realities of life.

Marie van Zyl had run not only off Stefanus Aucamp's farm and after that out of Gawie Steyn's house but also, ultimately, out of the story that Louis Wassenaar had shown Mavis Smith. And she had entered into the realities of the rooms and passages of Kandora House. And, of course, there is nothing singular about all this. It is only the way life is. How often does it not happen to you? You walk out of the insignificance of a story and find yourself in the midst of a warm and turbulent and meaningful life.

Mrs McAfa, the caretaker of Kandora House, opened the door of her room a matter of about six inches, in response to the knock that came after dark. She looked with marked disfavour at the young woman with the fair hair standing before her. She also sniffed significantly, to let the young woman know (if she had been drinking) that Mrs McAfa had detected the fact. This was all bluff, of course. Mrs McAfa, who drank gin steadily throughout the waking hours of each day, was never in a condition to tell from their breath if other people had been drinking.

"You ain't got no suitcase," Mrs McAfa observed.

"I – I lost my suitcase," Marie van Zyl replied. "A man chased me down the street and I got scared and I dropped my suitcase and I run. That's how I got here."

"Chased you?" Mrs McAfa enquired. "Chased you out of his room, most likely. My terms is twenty-seven and six a week, in advance. Furnished, service and coffee."

"I haven't got quite that," Marie van Zyl answered, feeling in her bag. "But I'll let you have the rest tomorrow."

Mrs McAfa pondered.

"You won't make that money in here," Mrs McAfa said. "Not from the men that comes here, you won't. Not them sort of men."

"I don't want them men," Marie van Zyl said, making an effort at seeming superior, but not succeeding very well because she was in a state bordering on physical exhaustion. "I got my own men. And I won't bring none of them here, neither."

"It's only because I got a kind heart," Mrs McAfa went on to explain. "And I knows what it is to be a girl on your own. How long you been in this game?"

"About two years," Marie van Zyl faltered. "I been a servant girl in

113

between, also." She didn't bother to think what she was answering. What was truth and what was lies. All she wanted at that moment was a bed to lie down on, and to stretch herself out on, and to have quiet where she could think. Or not even think.

Mrs McAfa opened the door and came out into the passage and began leading the way up the noisome staircase on to the landing on the first floor. A long row of rooms, each with a window and with unwashed panes and a greasy-looking door opening on to the veranda. In most of the rooms lights were burning. Through the sketchy curtains Marie van Zyl could see. . .

[Bosman never completed this story]

The Clay-pit

ALTHOUGH it happened so many years ago, anybody in Zeerust can still tell you the story of Diederik Uys and Johanna Greyling and old Bertus Pienaar. And when they mention certain events that happened at the clay-pit where Bertus was making bricks for the new house that he never built, people in Zeerust will declare that they can still go and point out that same spot to you – as though it is all just something of yesterday. They don't explain that earth and stones have been washed into that depression by many rains, and that tall weeds cover the site of the clay-pit, like a grave on a farm that has passed into the hands of strangers.

And whoever tells you the story will always add, at the end of it, that even though Diederik Uys was guilty he should never have been hanged. You will also be told that what actually hanged Diederik Uys was a strand of Johanna Greyling's hair, that was of a wanton colour, yellow, not unlike the colour of a hangman's rope if you were to tease out the ends.

Whereas the truth is that her hair was not always light.

Anyway, you can see from this that the incidents linking together the fortunes of the young bywoner, Diederik Uys, and of the young girl, Johanna Greyling, and of the ageing Bertus Pienaar made a good story, that was told over and over again. Otherwise each person who tells this story would not be able to bring in that touch about the hangman's rope so confidently. A high school girl, home for the holidays, would otherwise not be able to talk of the strings in a hangman's noose as familiarly as though it were crochet thread.

Bertus Pienaar and his wife were both past middle age and childless when they adopted a girl of ten from the Church orphanage in Kimberley. This action of theirs aroused a good deal of discussion at the time. It was not unreasonable that Bertus Pienaar and his wife should have decided to adopt a child who would continue, on their Bushveld farm, from where they would one day have to leave off. But then you would have expected them to adopt a man-child, still young enough to be bent in the way he should grow. He would need to have a strong voice and sturdy legs, which were more important than broad shoulders, since these would develop naturally with the responsibilities that went with a 6 000-morgen farm. His features, also, must not be too sharp; nor his eyes too thoughtful. Else he might grow of a sudden restive, some morning when there would be a low wind in the maroelas.

No doubt Bertus Pienaar and his wife new exactly, when they went to the orphanage, what was the kind of child that they desired to adopt. But because their lives had been in more than one way barren they were perhaps not surprised, in the moment of making their choice, to find that they had picked, instead, a small, dark-haired girl who had a ready smile, and about whose parents the matron could tell them nothing.

Some years later Bertus Pienaar's wife died.

And not long after that people in the Bushveld began to shake their heads at the way that Bertus was treating his adopted daughter.

Since Bertus Pienaar was known to be a God-fearing man, a good deal could be overlooked about the manner that he saw fit to discipline Johanna Greyling after she had left school and was passing through the stage of childhood into young womanhood.

It was said of old Bertus Pienaar, also, that in his dealings with his neighbours he was not a hard man. That was one reason why, for instance, his singular action after Johanna Greyling's confirmation did not make more talk. At her catechism Johanna wore a white frock that was so showy that it might almost have been made of silk. Only, everybody knows, of course, that silk is black. And Johanna looked so comely in that white frock that the predikant did not even notice when she gave the wrong answer to the first question, "Whence do you know your wretchedness?" Whereas every member of the confirmation class knew that the answer was, "Out of the word of God."

Yet, when she came back to the farm, Bertus made Johanna take off that frock, that must have cost him the price of quite a number of sheep-skins. And he straightway went and thrust the dress into the flames of the bread-oven at the side of the house.

A neighbour, Oupa van Tonder, a man who used few words but those usually the right ones, commented on Bertus Pienaar's actions thus:

"Bertus has got a queer idea of a wardrobe," Oupa van Tonder said.

At that time everybody in the Marico knew that Johanna Greyling had no more than two frocks, which she wore on alternate weeks. It was also known that there were wash-days on which Bertus Pienaar would stride across to where Johanna was kneeling beside the bath-tub by the dam and would correct her with the end of a sjambok laid across her shoulders. Several Marico farmers, driving past the dam on their way to Ramoutsa, had actually seen Bertus Pienaar administering instruction to his daughter in that fashion.

It was only on account of the esteem, of a long-standing nature, in which Bertus Pienaar was held by the Dwarsberg community that some farmer did not pull up his mule-team and, having tied the reins to the off-wheel, go over to the dam and lay the doubled thongs of the sjambok across Bertus Pienaar's shoulder-blades, instead.

Part of this esteem was due to Bertus's piety and deep love of religion. The other part of it arose from the fact that, although past middle life, he was still agile on his feet. And when teaching a kaffir not to let the cattle stray into the lucerne lands Bertus would always first draw back two paces and then charge forward with the whole weight of his body behind his fist. Once Bertus found it necessary also to teach a kaffir not to leave half the mealies on the cobs in shelling them. The doctor who came to attend the kaffir said that he did not think that even a charging rhinoceros could have taught the kaffir as well as Bertus had done. The doctor said that after he had counted the number of stitches.

Consequently, when Johanna Greyling ran away from Bertus Pienaar to Diederik Uys, a bywoner in his early twenties living on an adjoining farm, there were many people in the Marico who were inclined to sympathise with the young couple.

In the end, however, Bertus Pienaar got Johanna Greyling back. Except that Bertus seemingly promised Diederik Uys that he would treat his adopted daughter less harshly in the future, little was known for sure as to what happened at that interview. Nevertheless, in places where farmers foregathered, many questions were asked, in the manner of one man speaking to another, as to why the young fellow Diederik Uys had let go of his girl so easily.

Shortly afterwards something else happened on Bertus Pienaar's farm that caused more discussion than ever. Bertus had had a clay-pit dug for bricks for his new house. And he made Johanna Greyling help tread the clay. The kaffirs poured buckets of water into the hole. Bertus Pienaar stood on the side of the pit with a long whip, driving half a dozen head of oxen round and round in the wet earth. And along with the cattle, the skirts of her print dress raised high, Johanna Greyling tramped in the red clay of the Transvaal.

The murder, a few days later, of Bertus Pienaar, caused less stir in the Marico than the fact of his having made his adopted daughter tread clay.

It was at daybreak that the kaffirs, coming to work with their buckets and spades, found their baas lying by the edge of the pit, with his face pressed deep into the hardening mud. Veldkornet Apie Nel, of the landdrost's office, was on the scene soon afterwards.

"They must have fought a long time in the night," Apie Nel said, surveying the area of grass that had been flattened by heavy boots. "They should rather have fought inside the clay-pit, Bertus and his murderer. They would then have kneaded up quite a lot of clay."

Veldkornet Nel spoke lightly. He had not much sympathy with Bertus Pienaar. And that was how most people felt about the matter. Old Bertus had got what was coming to him, people said.

They also believed that that was why Apie Nel allowed several months to go by before he went over to the whitewashed rondavel of Diederik Uys, one afternoon, and, discoursing on matters of no greater earnestness than the rust in the late wheat sowings, took Diederik Uys into custody. But why Apie Nel had waited so long was because he had hoped that in some way Diederik Uys would betray his guilt. He was a deep one, Apie Nel, and he had much patience.

Meanwhile, Johanna Greyling had again run away. And this time there had been no one to fetch her back to the farm. It was learnt a little later that she had got as far as Kimberley, where she obtained employment of a sort.

She must have run pretty fast along the transport road to Kimberley, with just two dresses and no money, people said, trying to be funny. For they knew that a young and attractive girl like Johanna Greyling would not have to wear out much shoe-leather in getting to Kimberley, transport drivers being what they were. Moreover, it was agreed that it was not just her sentimental memories of the orphanage in Kimberley that had served to draw Johanna back to the diamond-mining town, with its dance-halls and saloons.

After Apie Nel had arrested Diederik Uys he searched his room, taking possession, among other things, of a tin locket that held a dark curl from Johanna Greyling's forehead. Afterwards Apie Nel returned the locket to his prisoner.

The veldkornet was in a difficult position. As things stood, there was so much public sympathy with Diederik Uys on account of Bertus Pienaar's unnatural usage of the girl, Johanna Greyling, that no Zeerust jury would bring in a verdict more stern than homicide, which would mean only a year or two of imprisonment. Such a verdict might have suited Diederik Uys. But it would not suit Veldkornet Apie Nel. A murder case came his way but rarely. Quite soon he would reach the age when he would have to retire. He would not be able to look back on his career with a proper kind of satisfaction if, at the end of it, he would have to admit that he had never succeeded in getting a white man hanged.

That was no doubt what caused the veldkornet to apply, through the public prosecutor, for a postponement of the trial of Diederik Uys until Johanna Greyling could be brought into court as a witness.

Johanna Greyling was subpoenaed. In court she said little. But when the coach that brought her back from Kimberley stopped in front of the Transvaal hotel, half the population of Zeerust saw her alight on to the pavement. The fate of Diederik Uys was sealed.

A woman like that, people said. And if in court Johanna Greyling spoke but few words, the Zeerust public had a good deal to say outside of the courthouse – and inside, too, in whispers.

Immediately all sympathy switched to the late Bertus Pienaar. People remembered that he had lived an upright and joyless life. And they said it was cowardly of a young fellow to go and suffocate an old man in the clay-pit, like that. They spoke as though Bertus Pienaar was a man who would allow just any passing stranger to push his face in the mud, and choke him in it, quietly.

They recalled how, after his wife's death, Bertus had tried to be both father and mother to Johanna Greyling, so that they spoke almost wistfully of the sjambok with which he sought to guide her along the right paths. And what was the thanks he got? – they asked.

For when Johanna Greyling stepped off the coach in Zeerust it was in the low-bosomed dress and the high heels of a harlot. And her cheeks were shamelessly painted the colour that old Bertus Pienaar's bricks would have been if he had had a chance to fire them in the kiln. And her hair was bleached the yellow of tamboekie grass in winter.

People had heard of abandoned women in the Kimberley dance-halls bleaching their hair. But this was the first time that Zeerust itself had been disgraced by the presence of such a woman. Everybody felt disgraced, including farmers who had come from many miles away just to look at her.

And that was why the lawyers of Diederik Uys put up so half-hearted a defence for their client in court. They knew there would be no mercy for a man who could have associated with such a woman. In the brazen presence of Johanna Greyling no juryman could pause to reflect that Diederik Uys had, after all, loved not a painted strumpet but a girl who had only two print dresses which she washed until they were threadbare.

I have often wondered what Diederik Uys thought, too, when he saw Johanna Greyling in court. And how he felt afterwards, in the solitude of his cell. I wonder what he thought when he opened the tin locket and gazed on that poor strand of dark hair inside – and realised that it no longer matched the bleached tresses of the Jezebel who had leaned on the rail of the witness box. But I feel that if he still remembered her as that farm girl who had once run away to him, then the hanging of Diederik Uys would, in the years to come, have been but a hollow triumph for Veldkornet Apie Nel.

Anyway, that is the story as it is to this day still told in Zeerust. One point, however, that everybody who tells the story seems to overlook is Bertus Pienaar's role in it, which was no less important for its having been so straightforward.

It is easy to see, in all Bertus Pienaar's actions, a thwarted passion for Johanna Greyling. And the fact that Diederik Uys did not at first seriously oppose Johanna's return to her adopted father's home shows that he had instinctively no fears in at least that respect. Diederik's letting her go like that was actually an insult to Bertus Pienaar.

Then there is Johanna Greyling. She must have had much of a sombre knowledge of life shut up inside her. Something as dark as that strand of hair enclosed in Diederik Uys's tin locket. Of course, Johanna Greyling knew at first hand that it was not she who had crossed Bertus Pienaar in his desire for her. She knew that it was his advancing age and not her virtue that stood between Bertus Pienaar and his passion. But it could not have brought ease to her smarting shoulder-blades – the knowledge that when her adopted father wielded the sjambok it was in the rage of impuissance.

One cannot pass by Johanna Greyling just lightly, somehow. Johanna Greyling, walking about the night streets of Kimberley, blonde-headed and with her high heels clicking on the pavement. Lifting her steps high as she had done in former days in the clay-pit of her adopted father.

"Onsterflike Liefde"

O N a lamp-post in front of the entrance to the Male Section of the Johannesburg Fort – as grim a prison as any that there is in the world – there is a placard in red letters announcing the forthcoming presentation of an Afrikaans play with the flaming title *Onsterflike Liefde* (Undying Love).

It seems a strange juxtaposition. What does one have to make of it? The placard with its flaring declaration that love is "onsterflik." And the prison gate. Two profound human realities. The prison gate stands at the entrance to a subterranean passage below an earthen rampart that is covered, significantly enough, with thorny cactus. Thick-stemmed symbolism. The stark aridities of the desert; a path bestrewn with thorns. Years ago, one remembers, those earthen ramparts of the Johannesburg Gaol were covered with a creeper that in the spring-time bore a wealth of magenta-hued blossoms which held a singular allurement for members of the public passing down Ameshoff Street. These bright-coloured flowers were obviously inappropriate and the prison authorities are to be congratulated on that strong insight into the ultimate realities of existence which led them to substitute spiny cactus.

And on the lamp-post, in front of the gaol, in red letters, the placard, *Onsterflike Liefde*. Here there is no incongruity, either. Love is also something that in its deepest essentials sits well with the desert and the thorns of the cactus, and has got very little to do with flowers. Love, in its deepest essentials, I have said. And love also stands as a gateway to those underground labyrinths of the human heart that are, alas, more tortuous than any of the passages twisting underneath the ramparts of the Fort. And more soulfully laden with the solemn intensities of life than are those passages. And more dark.

And passing by that prison gate and that placard on the lamp-post the other day I pondered on a story that in its human qualities would not be in any way different from any one of the thousands of other stories which have had their setting at the entrance gate to the Male Section of the Johannesburg Fort. I thought of the feelings of a girl coming out of that gate from a visit to her man locked behind bars Perhaps he had already been sentenced. Perhaps he was awaiting trial. That did not matter. What mattered was that when she left she had given him that promise which every woman makes to every man whom she visits in a prison. She would wait for him for ever Through how many dust-laden centuries have women not made the same promise, in the same tone of voice, under these same circumstances. And in how many languages. Babylonian, Phrygian, Cappadocian, Visi-Gothic, Sesotho.

And this girl, stepping out on to the pavement in front of the Johannesburg Fort, into sudden sunshine, hearing the prison gate clanging shut behind her, and remembering or forgetting that her last words were a promise of undying love to a man: and her eyes encounter that placard pasted on the lamp-post, *Onsterflike Liefde* Whether she is going to break that promise or whether she will keep it seems a matter almost of less significance than the fact that in the words she has just uttered she has become one with all those other women.

Although she doesn't know it, she is no longer an isolated individual. She has become absorbed into a tradition that goes back to before the dawn of civilisation, to before Minos, and to before Assyria and to before Troy. By the words she has uttered she has become an initiate, whether she likes it or not, into a female fellowship that has a heritage that is both proud and tarnished, and from whose bonds there is no escape. Whether she keeps or breaks the promise she has made to her man makes no difference, for in either event she will merely be acting in accordance with ancient tradition And if the man behind the bars of the Johannesburg Gaol happen to be the last, so far, of a long line of her lovers, she also happen to be the last, so far, in a long line of a strange and gaudy and battered sisterhood.

So it doesn't matter if this girl steps out on the pavement and doesn't even notice the placard about *Onsterflike Liefde* because she is busy thinking about some other man. Or if what comes into her mind is the recollection that the pineapple pump of the milk-bar counter behind which she works is nearly empty.

It is all part of the same barbarically ornamented magnificence o life. And who shall say that life is not magnificent?

Underworld

ENDRIK asked me what was on my mind. And so I told him that I was wanting to turn out a story, and I couldn't think of what to write.

"The grass is yellow on the other side of the Dwarsberge," Hendrik said, "and the last moepels fell from the trees at least a month ago. But there were tents on the kerkplein at Zeerust when I was there last. Can't you write some more about Nagmaal?"

But I said that I wanted no part in the Marico Bushveld any more. The Marico was getting too civilised, I said. They were ploughing the mealie-lands with tractors; and several Marico farmers were already beginning to attach more value to their homemade riempies benches, of stinkwood and tamboetie, than to the chesterfield suites in the Johannesburg furniture-dealers' catalogues. Civilisation was making deep inroads into the Marico, I said. I wanted something more primitive.

"I have decided that I want to write about the underworld," I said. "About how the other half lives. I want to write about Fordsburg: two crooks sitting in a café discussing some criminal project – and a detective in the corner, with a newspaper in front of him, watching them. I want the seamy side of existence. Life naked and in the raw. I want to depict the cesspool, in other words. Squalor. And green slime floating on the surface; and all the stark things hidden underneath. But that isn't all. I want also to record eternal truths in terms of humanity: the red blood of humanity pulsing in warm and strange and terrible beauty under all the – "

"I see," Hendrik answered. "And so you want to write about Fordsburg. But then why don't you?"

"I can't think what to write," I said. "I want a story. And it won't come. I want blood. Above all, blood. You see, I know Fordsburg, all right. I have canvassed advertising there. And if you have ever canvassed advertising you'll know what I mean by sordid – "

"I have in my time sold vacuum-cleaners," Hendrik responded, briefly. "But come, let us repair to Fordsburg. We'll find lots of stories there. I have lived in Fordsburg."

So we grabbed up a pile of copy paper and some pencils and we set out.

On our way down in the elevator we informed the liftman of our quest.

"Yes," the liftman said, "Fordsburg is the place, all right. Go to John Ware Park, where all those down and outs are. I can tell you a story about John Ware Park and a gold bar. It's a story I heard some years ago."

Unfortunately, however, the liftman couldn't tell us the story. There wasn't any time. We didn't have enough floors to go down. We hurried up Eloff Street, past the Grand Hotel, and then down President Street to the Mayfair tram stop. At the Grand Hotel corner I saw a tall, thin girl with blue eyes. She seemed aloof, somehow, and mysterious. What enhanced her air of mystery was the circumstance of one of her eyes being more blue than the other. Did God do that, or a jealous male? I didn't know. But for a moment I wondered whether we wouldn't get a better story from that girl than from the underworld suburb of Fordsburg.

I dismissed that idea, however. I felt that that girl could have given us only an O. Henry story. Sky-blue. The colour that God made her eyes. The blue from a short left jab to the optic. A story about God and man. This has always been a source of distress to me – the fact that life tells only O. Henry stories.

The tram clanged and rolled towards the Fordsburg dip. We passed John Ware Park. No good. It was the coldest day of the year and John Ware Park's last tramp was obviously already many miles on the road to Durban.

So Hendrik and I went into a pub, instead.

"This is the second-oldest hotel in Johannesburg," Hendrik announced when we got into the lounge. "The oldest hotel is diagonally across the way from here."

"It must have been a grand place in its time," I remarked, when we had seated ourselves at a little table near the door, and had ordered drinks. "Look at all the heavy woodwork. And the imposing looking arches above the doorways. And all that oak panelling."

"It's all steeped in history," Hendrik replied, "the early days of Johannesburg. I bet those stains on the ceiling are at least half a century old."

We flung the pile of copy paper on to the table and sat back. We could take notes later, when the lounge filled up with the denizens of Fordsburg's underworld. At the moment the place was almost deserted.

Time passed. We had several drinks.

The proprietor came and spoke to us. In a moment we guessed what he was thinking. So I thought I would explain. I indicated the pile of copy paper in front of us.

"We have come here for atmosphere," I said. "We want to write a story or two. Local colour and all that, you know. Raw life."

"Yes," the proprietor answered, "you'll get it here. I can tell you a story about some illicit gold bars. It happened in John Ware Park some years ago – "

And all the time Hendrik and I could sense that in his conversing with us the proprietor was delivering himself of a set speech. We could feel that whatever he said to us was by way of being a leg-pull. And, of course, we knew why.

We had taken up a position facing the door. From where we were seated we could study the variegated pattern of humanity that we expected to see floating in and out of the place – and which didn't float. But the proprietor had summed us up as a couple of detectives who were investigating some crime or other and who were on the lookout for a suspect. The paper and the pencils were a blind. We could see from the proprietor's manner that it wasn't the first time that a couple of detectives had walked into that lounge in the guise of writers looking for copy.

When the proprietor turned away Hendrik and I laughed.

"I suppose the detectives are even more obvious about it," I said to Hendrik, "when they come in here and pretend to be writers. No doubt, what a detective would pull out of his pocket would be a reporter's notebook. You know the kind of thing I mean. A little writing-pad that you buy at a stationer's and that has got printed on it in bold, clear type: 'Reporter's Notebook.' What reporter is ever going to carry a thing like that around with him when he can grab up a fistful of copy paper any time he likes? And I suppose that when a detective comes in here, pretending to be a writer, he actually even writes."

For by this time it had become abundantly clear to both Hendrik and myself that we would have no use for our pencils, that day. There was nothing that we could make notes about. Unless we wanted to describe the interior of the lounge that had once been the palatial rendezvous of Rand millionaires and that, in spite of half a century of neglect, could still reveal, in the opulence of architrave and cornice and mantel, a grandeur that had not faded in the mere process of Fordsburg having declined into slumdom.

Hendrik grabbed up the copy paper and thrust it back into the pocket of his overcoat.

"I'll say that at least this much is new to me," he remarked. "A detec tive diverting suspicion from himself by posing as a writer. I have unt now only known of a detective posing as a reader: as the reader of newspaper over the top of which he gazes steadily at the person he i going to put handcuffs on."

But Hendrik and I were both beginning to feel – without having th courage to say as much to each other, openly – that we weren't collect ing much in the way of a story of Johannesburg's underworld in thes licensed premises that for fifty years had refused to grow shabby. An just then two men came into the lounge. They came and sat near us. On man had long, thin features and looked anaemic; the other was fat an full-faced and wore an open-necked shirt. They ordered brandies.

I looked significantly at Hendrik. He pulled the copy paper out o his pocket in one hit.

"We'll take down everything they say," I said in low tones to Hen drik. "I understand their talk. They call a detective a 'john', and thei word for an arrest is a 'pinch'; they also refer to a prison warder as 'screw' – and they say – "

"You seem to have learnt a hell of a lot here in Fordsburg," Hendri said, with what seemed like a sneer, "canvassing advertising."

These two men, the fat-faced one and the one with the long an somewhat rat-like features, spoke together, first in whispers and after wards in normal tones. We could hear quite distinctly what they saic But we did not make notes of their talk.

"I'll do my best," the thin-faced man said, "but it will be difficult fo me to get your son through matric this year, especially as he faile J. C. in both physics and Latin. I could coach him for a couple of hour every day after school. No, if I were you, I wouldn't bother about let ting him take that correspondence course."

"We'll go to the hotel on the other side of the road," Hendrik saic "It's even older. And it's got even more atmosphere."

"And more respectability," I said, "and more venerable traditions Instead of matric they will probably be discussing fourth-year divinit I feel we better go back to the office. That liftman in our building, now Perhaps we can ride up and down in the lift long enough, and he'll tel us that story of the gold bars in John Ware Park."

But, because we had had a few drinks, we didn't land in that othe and older hotel straight away. Instead, we walked into a butcher-shop

The blockman wanted to take our order.

I told him what we had come for. We wanted blood, I said. Blood.

But the blockman expressed his regret. They had just scattered fresh sawdust on the floor and with the meat shortage all he could offer us was bully-beef and Vienna sausages. There was no blood in the whole shop, he said. Perhaps we had come to the wrong suburb. . .

So we went into that other and older and more sumptuous Fordsburg hotel, instead. And when we passed through the portals we took off our hats, and in our gesture there was an old-world stateliness.

Inside the lounge of this hotel we looked at the wainscotting, and then at the ceiling, that was like the interior of an Elizabethan manor house. But most of all Hendrik and I were in awe of the bar. Because the pedestal of the bar, just behind the brass rail, and all the way round, was faced with Italian marble. It was the kind of marble that fifty years ago had got quarried to form the base of a pulpit in a church. And this marble had been incorporated into the pedestal of the bar of what in the early days had been Johannesburg's show hotel.

During the course of fifty years the brass rail had got worn through in parts by the feet of the patrons. Parts of the brass-work had also been replaced with steel. But the marble remained. It was sullied and battered, but it was good for another thousand years. Sounding brass wears out, as St. Paul has proclaimed. But you never replace marble.

My gaze was attracted to one of the customers. He wore a long white beard and his face was deeply furrowed. But he also looked good for lifting his arm another thousand years at that same bar counter. And I realised that his foot had been resting on that rail for the same number of years that the Italian marble had been secured into position behind it. I realised that this ancient patron was as battered as the marble behind the foot-rail of the bar – and that he was as irremoveable. . .

Some time later Hendrik and I withdrew from this hotel in Fordsburg, also. And because it was getting late into the afternoon we took the tram back home.

"Mind you, Fordsburg is the place to get real inside dope about the underworld," Hendrik said to me after the conductor had taken our fares. "We were just unlucky today, I suppose."

"I don't know about underworld," I said. "To me it was more like old-world. With all this history and tradition it was like a visit to Stratford-on-Avon. They ought to call it Ye Olde Fordesburg. Perhaps we should have gone to John Ware Park, after all."

"If it hadn't been so cold," Hendrik reminded me.

"If it hadn't been so cold," I agreed.

And just because it was so cold, when we got back into Eloff Street we decided to go and have a quick one at the Grand Hotel. And it was near there, somewhere, that I again saw that girl with the blue eyes, one darker than the other, and I again wondered if we shouldn't have followed her instead. It would have been funny if she had led us to John Ware Park, I thought. . .

But Hendrik was already going up the steps into the Grand Hotel. And we went into the lounge and sat down at a table and called for brandies. And there were two men sitting at the table next to us. I noticed the fat one particularly. His red neck, and his white expanse of shirt, and the diamond pin glistening under his collar.

The two men conversed in low tones. But afterwards I could hear what they were saying. The man with the diamond pin was doing the talking.

"If Snowy don't get here by three," he said, "it means he's been pinched dead to rights. And a couple of smacks on the ear with a piece of hosepipe will make him squawk. We better beat it before the johns get on our trail over that gold bar."

Then their conversation once more became inaudible.

"There seems to be something in the wind," Hendrik said.

Something in the wind. . .

I thought of the wind whirling a handful of dried leaves around in the deserted John Ware Park. And I thought of a piece of paper fluttering in the wind above the Zeerust kerkplein, after the last Nagmaal visitor had trekked away. And I heard the newspaper crackling in the hands of the fat man's confederate – the newspaper over the top of which he was peering very intently.

Notes on the Text

T HE Herman Charles Bosman Papers held at the Harry Ransom Humanities Research Center in Austin, Texas, were consulted extensively in the process of preparing this volume. With only five exceptions ("The Night-dress", "In Church", "Politics and Love", "Veld Story" and "'Onsterflike Liefde'"), original typescripts were used as source texts for the stories that make up this collection. This does not mean that the typescripts were followed slavishly, however. Where the published version of a particular story contained improvements on the original, or corrected what were clearly errors in the original, I have incorporated these amendments. In all cases an effort was made to provide versions that are as close as possible to the author's intentions (as reflected in his typescripts) while taking due cognisance of improvements contained in later published versions. Where two or more typescript versions of a particular story exist, I followed the last version.

One otherwise puzzling detail in these stories requires clarification. The closing remark in "Politics and Love" is a contemporary (1950s) reference to the division of Korea into two states (at the 38th Parallel) and the accompanying rise in hostility between North and South.

The source texts that were used for this edition are listed below in alphabetical order. Details of first publication (where applicable) have also been supplied. An asterisk indicates a previously unpublished story.

"The Affair at Ysterspruit." Undated typescript, Harry Ransom Humanities Research Center. First published in Afrikaans as "Die Voorval by Ijzerspruit", *Die Ruiter* 1.48 (2 Apr 1948): 7, 43; in English in *Unto Dust* (1963): 121–126.

"A Boer Rip van Winkel." Undated typescript, HRHRC. First published in *Unto Dust* (1963): 154–160.

"The Clay-pit." Undated typescript, HRHRC. First published in *Unto Dust* (1963): 113–120.

* "The Heart of a Woman." Undated typescript, HRHRC; title supplied.

"In Church." *The Sjambok* 2.38 (2 Jan 1931): 16.

* "Jakob's Trek." Undated typescript, HRHRC; title supplied.

"Louis Wassenaar." Undated typescript, HRHRC. First published in *Bosman's Johannesburg* (1986): 114–137.

"The Murderess." Undated typescript, HRHRC. First published in *Personality* 31 July 1969: 24–28.

"New Elder." Undated typescript, HRHRC. First published in *Personality* 25 Sept 1969: 75, 77.

"The Night-dress." *The Sjambok* 2.44 (13 Feb 1931): 16.

* "Night on the Veld." Undated typescript, HRHRC; title supplied.

* "The Old Muzzle-loader." Undated typescript, HRHRC; title supplied.

"Old Transvaal Story." Undated typescript, HRHRC. First published as "The Transvaal Murder Story" in *On Parade* 3 Sept 1948: 8–9.

"'Onsterflike Liefde.'" *The South African Opinion* Apr 1944: 12–13.

"Politics and Love." *The Forum* 13.54 (6 Apr 1951): 14.

"Shy Young Man." Undated typescript, HRHRC. First published in *Personality* 25 Sept 1969: 78.

"A Tale Writ in Water." Undated typescript, HRHRC. First published in *Selected Stories* (1980): 142–146.

"Underworld." Undated typescript, HRHRC. First published in *Selected Stories* (1980): 147–152.

"Veld Story." *The South African Opinion* Jan 1946: 10–11.

The essay, "The South African Short Story Writer", first appeared as by 'One of Them' in *Trek* Oct 1948: 24–25. The note on W. W. Jacobs first appeared as "The Art of W. W. Jacobs" in *The South African Opinion* 12 Dec 1936: 20. The note on W. C. Scully is an extract from "Aspects of South African Literature", *Trek* Sept 1948: 24. The first paragraph of the note on Pauline Smith comes from the same source, while the rest originally appeared as "The Truth of the Veld" (a review of *The Little Karoo*) in *The South African Opinion* Apr 1945: 24, 31. The preface to *Veld-trails and Pavements* (ed. Bosman and C. Bredell; Johannesburg: A. P. B., 1949) is reproduced in its entirety.